# Final Run

# James Pattinson

© James Pattinson 1977
James Pattinson has asserted his rights under the Copyright, Design and Patents Act, 1988, to be identified as the author of this work.

First published in 1977 by Robert Hale Limited.

This edition published in 2018 by Endeavour Media Ltd.

# Table of Contents

| | |
|---|---|
| Chapter One – Foundation | 5 |
| Chapter Two – Hardware | 14 |
| Chapter Three – Business Talk | 23 |
| Chapter Four – A Man Called Alvarez | 34 |
| Chapter Five – Night Drive | 42 |
| Chapter Six – Surprise From Father Rubello | 52 |
| Chapter Seven – Of A Sort | 62 |
| Chapter Eight – Four-Letter Word | 72 |
| Chapter Nine – Idyllic | 83 |
| Chapter Ten – Shopping List | 91 |
| Chapter Eleven – The Room | 103 |
| Chapter Twelve – A Word With Captain Varco | 112 |
| Chapter Thirteen – Joe | 122 |
| Chapter Fourteen – Word Of Advice | 128 |
| Chapter Fifteen – A Sack Of Money | 133 |
| Chapter Sixteen – Money To Burn | 140 |

# Chapter One – Foundation

'It could make you a rich man,' Korvan said.

Blade lifted an eyebrow. 'Rich?'

'Comparatively speaking. Rich compared with what you are now. It could set you on your feet; give you a foundation to build on; working capital. Isn't that what you want?'

Blade looked at him, trying to spot the catch. Because there had to be one, and maybe more than one; a load of catches. It was surely not going to be quite as easy as it was being made to sound. With Korvan on the other end of the deal that stood to reason.

He was not at all sure he liked the man. In fact, when he came to think about it, he was quite sure he did not. Korvan had a narrow head covered with tight little curls of black hair, except at the sides where there was a touch of grey. His face was lean, deeply furrowed from cheekbone to chin, the nose prominent and slightly curving like the beak of a bird of prey. His eyes gave an impression of opacity; looking into them was like trying to see through a window of frosted glass, impossible to tell what was on the other side. His mouth opened scarcely at all when he spoke; the words came out like convicts escaping from prison through a narrow breach in the walls. He was about five feet eight inches tall and had a compact build; with his expensive, well-fitting clothes he put Blade in mind of a neatly tied parcel, very sharp at the edges and with no loose ends showing.

Korvan had, so Blade understood, been born somewhere in Central Europe, but nobody appeared to know which particular part. He never talked about that early period of his life; it was something he seemed to prefer to forget. His English was precise and correct, but he spoke it with a marked foreign accent. The accent, however, had proved no handicap in his adopted country: he had done well for himself, that was obvious at a glance; he had the look of a really prosperous man. Blade would have liked to be as prosperous as Korvan looked, but he doubted whether he ever would be; there was a certain knack required in the making of money, and he had never had the knack.

'It could make me a dead man,' he said. 'Six feet of ground isn't my idea of a good foundation to build on. Nobody's rich in the grave.'

'King Tut was,' Dancey said; and he gave a high-pitched laugh, as if he had made a big, big joke.

Blade refused even to smile; he just stared at Dancey very coldly.

'You think that's funny?'

'Well, what's wrong with you?' Dancey sounded faintly aggrieved. 'Ain't you got no sense of humour?'

'Maybe I haven't. Or maybe it just happens to be a different brand from yours.'

Dancey was not at all like Korvan. He was clumsy and shapeless, like a figure made out of modelling clay by an unskilled child. He had heavy features and large hands and feet, and there was plenty of muscle about him even if some of it had started turning to fat. His hair was thinning, but what there was of it he grew long so that it hung like a rather frayed and greasy curtain over the back of his collar. There was a wart on his upper lip and a scar under his left eye.

'You can keep your jokes,' Blade told him.

They were sitting in Korvan's library, which he also used as an office. Tall windows looked out on to a wide expanse of shaven grass flanked by trees and shrubs, and a gardener could be seen doing some work on a bed of roses. Korvan's house was in Surrey; there was a farm attached to it, but that was simply a rich man's plaything; he employed a manager to run it, and if it lost money he was not likely to worry. Blade guessed that in fact it probably made a healthy profit like everything else Korvan touched, even though the profit might be chicken-feed compared with the yield from other projects — like the one he had in mind now, for instance.

'You're not going to be killed,' Korvan said. 'What use would a dead man be to me?'

'Do I get a guarantee of that?'

There was a cynical twist to Korvan's mouth. 'What do you want? Life insurance?'

'Why would I be interested in life insurance? I've got no dependants.'

'Nobody you'd like to leave some money to? Like a friend perhaps? Or a woman?'

'I don't make friends,' Blade said, 'and the last woman walked out on me when I couldn't pay the rent any more.'

Korvan gave a slight shake of the head. 'You really are a loner, aren't you, Frankie? When are you going to settle down, make a home for yourself?'

'If people like me settled down and made homes for themselves where would people like you find agents to do their dirty work?'

Korvan looked pained. 'Don't talk like that. You make it sound like something illegal.'

'You mean it isn't?' Blade said.

'Of course it's not. It's a straightforward business transaction, nothing more nor less.'

'Straightforward?'

'We'll not be breaking any laws. Not in this country, anyway.'

'But we could be in some other country? Is that it?'

'Well, who knows what laws other countries have? We can't be expected to make a study of every legal system in the world before we enter into financial negotiations.'

'They might expect it all the same; the countries concerned,' Blade said, but he did not pursue the matter because there was no point in doing so; talking about it would not alter the situation. 'So why did you pick on me? Why me rather than somebody else?'

'Because you seemed to be the right man for the job. You know that part of the world. You speak the language. You're capable.'

'There must be others who could fill the bill just as well.'

'That's possible,' Korvan admitted. 'But why should I bother to go looking for anyone else when you're available?'

'What makes you think I'm available?'

Korvan made a small gesture of impatience. 'You are surely not going to pretend you're not?'

Blade let it go. Korvan knew the score.

'Besides,' Korvan said, 'I want a man I can trust. There are far too many swindlers and double-crossers knocking around.'

Blade gave a sardonic laugh. 'Don't talk to me about trust. The only reason you think you can count on me is because I need the money. I can't afford to go off the rails, and you know it.'

Korvan shook his head. 'You take too cynical a view; there are other reasons. You have a reputation for honesty — of a sort. You never double-crossed anyone — not that I heard of.'

'That's true. It's maybe why I'm still around after thirty-five years of life on this planet.'

'And no scars either,' Dancey put in. 'No broken bones nor nothing.'

'I wouldn't say that. Not quite.'

Dancey gave him a careful inspection. 'I don't see nothing. You look okay to me.'

'Bones mend. Scars don't necessarily show — except when you strip down.'

'So you've had trouble?'

'I've had trouble.'

'Haven't we all?' Korvan said. 'It's a part of life. No need to go into that.'

'Let's go into something else, then. Figures. How much do I stand to get?'

'Shall we say ten thousand pounds? How does that appeal to you?'

It appealed to Blade very much, but he did not say so. He just said: 'You think ten thousand is going to make me a rich man? After all the galloping inflation we've been having.'

'I did say comparatively speaking. Ten thousand is not to be sniffed at even these days.'

'I'm not sniffing at it.'

Korvan helped himself to a cigar from a box on his big mahogany desk and clipped off the end. Dancey got up quickly to light it for him. Korvan puffed smoke into the air. He did not offer the cigars to Blade, or, for that matter, to Dancey. Possibly he thought they would not appreciate the qualities of a fine cigar.

'And after all,' he continued, 'what is it you have to do? What does it amount to? Just to make contact with these people and arrange the deal.'

'Suppose they don't want to do a deal?'

'But they do; they do.'

'How do you know?'

'They were the ones who put out feelers. Through certain channels, you understand.'

'Why can't you complete the deal through those channels?'

'That would not be practical. There has to be closer contact. They will only make the final arrangements with my personal representative. You.'

'If I take the job.'

'I think you'll take it,' Korvan said.

Blade thought so too; it was far too good an offer to turn down, even though there was certainly going to be plenty of risk attached, whatever Korvan might say to the contrary.

'Maybe you'd better give me a few more details,' he said. 'About the merchandise; about how it's to be delivered; that sort of thing.'

Korvan gave him some details, and Blade could see the risk growing minute by minute. Well, what else could you expect? Why else would the rate for the job be as much as ten thousand pounds?

'How are they going to make payment?' he asked. 'Through a Swiss bank? By credit transfer?'

Korvan shook his head. 'These people don't go in for that kind of thing. In money matters it seems they're inclined to be rather primitive. They wish to pay in cash. American dollars. You will collect.'

Blade saw more trouble looming ahead. So he had to carry a load of money away with him. Hot money. It was true Korvan had not actually said it would be hot, but of course it had to be.

'That's another reason why I have to employ an agent I can trust,' Korvan said. 'Some people might simply vanish with the takings.'

'You think I won't?'

'If I didn't feel sure of that, would I be talking to you now? Would I have offered you the job?'

'I suppose not. You're sure these people will have the money?'

'Oh, they'll have it all right. Don't worry your head about that.'

'How did they get it? Rob a bank?'

Korvan smiled. 'Do you know, Frankie? I wouldn't be at all surprised.'

Blade could not be certain whether he was serious or not. He could have been joking, but somehow it hardly sounded like a joke; far from it.

There were a lot of warning bells sounding off inside Blade's head, a full battery of them. And they carried one message; they were telling him not to go any further with the proposition, not another step; telling him that he was bound to regret it later if he did; telling him to pull out now while he still had the chance. He was getting the message all right; he was getting it very loud and very clear; but it was not going to make a bit of difference for all that, because there was too much pressure the other way. For suppose he did pull out; where else could he lay his hands on the kind of money that Korvan was offering? Times were hard and likely to become harder for a man like him, a rolling stone, an adventurer with no solid foundation of trade or profession.

# Final Run

There had been a time, long past, when he appeared committed to a career in the world of insurance; safe, assured, permanent, with progressive rises in salary and gradual promotion in a mammoth company of which he could never hope to be more than a very small, if useful part; a cog in a vast, impersonal machine. At the age of twenty-three he had taken a long, hard look ahead and had not been happy with the view that had presented itself to him. Forty more years of travelling to the office in the morning and home again in the evening; marriage to the girl with whom he had drifted into a half-hearted engagement; a house being paid for month by month through a building society; a car on the never-never, to be washed and polished at weekends; a rented colour television set; a package holiday in Spain or Majorca, or maybe Yugoslavia or Greece, once a year; retirement and a pension after completing the course; and finally perhaps a slab of chiselled marble over his coffin or a tasteful urn for his ashes. Holy smoke!

He was appalled by the prospect; he almost gave a yelp of dismay. Was that to be his life? No more than that? Like hell, it was.

He chucked the job; he broke off the engagement. There were tears, tantrums, recriminations. She was nineteen, blonde, soft, a real dolly; there were thousands more like her, dressing the same way, having the same tastes, the same standards, dreaming the same dreams, wanting the same things; the advertisers saw to that. He looked at her with that same cold, clear vision with which he had stared into the future, and he saw what she would be like in ten or twenty years' time; the increasing fat, the sagging chin, the dolly gradually turning into the old doll.

Again he recoiled from the prospect; again he saw the pit opening in front of him, the pit into which he had almost stumbled and from which he had drawn back only just in time.

'You lied to me,' she said, her voice shrill with accusation. 'You said you loved me. You don't. You never really did.'

He made no attempt to deny it, to protest that she was wrong. What she had said was the truth. He might for a while have imagined that he was in love with her, but it had never been real; there had been a certain physical attraction, sensual, nothing more; it was not enough to serve as the foundation of a lifetime of being together, not nearly enough.

'I hate you,' she said. 'My God, how I hate you.'

'Then it's as well we're breaking it off, isn't it? Hate is no basis for a happy marriage.'

She looked ready to hit him. 'That's right; make a joke of it; that's all it is to you. You're no better than an animal. You never meant to marry me; you just promised to so you could have me. I should have known.'

She was wrong there; if there had been any seduction it had been as much on her side as on his; she had been as ready for it as he had. But there was no point in arguing over that.

He told her he was giving up the insurance job and going away, and she said that was just fine because she never wanted to see him again as long as she lived; the sight of him made her sick. She was certainly cut up about it; it had hurt her pride to discover that he did not want her any more; he could see that clearly enough. But he knew she would get over it, and she did; six months later she was married to a man named Ogg, a door-to-door salesman working for a firm of brush manufacturers. Blade encountered her some years later with a brood of budding Oggs on whom the imprint of the father was stamped like a trademark, poor little devils.

He had just come back from Singapore, deeply tanned, lean and rangy as a greyhound, his hair bleached to the colour of barley straw. He saw the way she looked at him with a quick appraisal, and he guessed she was thinking of what it might have been like if she had been married to him instead of Ogg; maybe wishing it had been so and regretting the way things had turned out. For his own part, he had no regrets; he wondered what he could ever have seen in her. She looked dowdy; she represented, he reflected, all the things he had run away from; and God, he was glad he had run.

'Nice to see you again,' he said. 'It's been a long time.'

'Five years,' she said without a moment's hesitation to work it out. 'And it's nice to see you, Frank.'

Maybe she had forgotten that she never wanted to see him again as long as she lived.

'How's the world treating you, Sylvia?'

The way the corners of her mouth went down told him all he needed to know about that. Maybe she was fed up with Ogg, fed up with looking after the little Oggs. Maybe Ogg was not bringing home enough money to keep up with the Joneses. That was something he himself was never going to have to worry about; he didn't even know the Joneses and didn't give a damn about keeping up with them. To hell with the Joneses, and the Smiths and the Browns and the Robinsons too, for that matter.

'You look as if you're doing well,' she said, with a trace of envy and possibly a little malice as well. 'What do you do for a living these days?'

'This and that. Anything that crops up.'

She suggested that they might go back to her house for coffee and a chat about old times, but he side-stepped the invitation; he had no desire to look at the Ogg nest, no wish to be drawn into a conversation that could become embarrassing for both of them; it was enough to have seen her, to have had a glimpse of the trap from which he had escaped.

He had not seen her since; the gap between his mode of living and hers could not have been wider. If he had told her about himself she would not have begun to understand, would have had no clue to the reasons why he should have chosen to live as he did. It was not, he had to admit, the kind of thing that would have appealed to every taste. A knife had grazed his ribs in Djakarta, a bullet nicked his ear in Manila; he had spent six weeks in a South African gaol, had been rescued from destitution in Buenos Aires by a night-club hostess who happened to like his face, had helped to build a dam in Nicaragua, worked on an oil-rig in Venezuela, been involved in a little local war in Guatemala and driven lorry-loads of gelignite over some of the worst roads in Central America.

At other times he had taken part in more lucrative, if scarcely less dangerous, projects. Operating on that treacherous ground where the margin between legality and illegality is no wider than the cutting edge of a razor, skating on the thinnest of thin ice, he had made a quick dollar here, a fast peso there, and had spent them with equal rapidity. Which was just fine if you never thought about the future, never asked yourself the question: 'Where do I go from here? What does it all lead to?'

But recently he had begun to ask himself just that. He had taken a good look at himself and had seen that he was not getting any younger, that he was not as much in love with this uncertain way of life as he had once been. And then the thought had come to him that maybe after all there was something to be said for the steady job, the home, the assured future.

He had thought about it a good deal lately and had come to the conclusion that what he needed was a bit of capital. With some capital he might start up a business, maybe get a partnership in something or other. Without capital he stood no chance of doing anything of the kind. Well, here was a useful ten thousand pounds waiting for him if he did this job for Korvan. It was not really enough, but maybe it would do. He was not terribly happy about the kind of job it was, but where else would he find anything to bring in that kind of money in so short a time? And he would make it the last operation; this one and no more; after this he was finished with the game, finished for good. He just hoped nothing would go wrong; he wanted the final run to be smooth and easy; no trouble, no alarms, just a straight business transaction. But he knew in his heart it would not be like that, because things never were. Nothing ever turned out to be quite as simple as it was supposed to be; not in his experience.

He looked at Korvan. 'And just how much cash do I have to collect from these people?'

'It could be a million dollars,' Korvan said.

## Chapter Two – Hardware

The signboards on the station proclaimed the fact that it was Quintuaquintzl, which had probably meant something to the original inhabitants of the place — and possibly had a meaning to some of the present inhabitants too — but was just a name to Blade. Nevertheless, it was the name he had been looking for; it told him that this was where he left the train.

He was not sorry to leave it; the journey had been slow and tedious, with stops at every station along the line. The seat had been hard and for much of the way he had been wedged too tightly for comfort between a large fat woman with greasy black hair and a hook-nosed man with high cheekbones and a coppery skin, neither of whom had spoken a word to him but had occasionally carried on a conversation across him, as though he had not been there. He had felt hot and sticky, and it had been even worse than the flight from London with the change of planes in Miami and Mexico City. It was just as well that this was to be the final run; he had lost all taste for this kind of business. Maybe he really was growing old.

He stepped down from the train into the brilliant sunlight, carrying all his luggage in his left hand. He was travelling light, with the minimum of spare clothing, the minimum of toilet gear; no camera, no field-glasses, none of the usual tourist's appendages to weight him down; everything he had fitted easily into the one much-used and ancient bag with the zip-fastener, which had accompanied him on all his journeying. And it was all he wanted; this was strictly a business trip and he was not sure where it might take him; but wherever it did, he was quite certain he would not wish to be lumbered with any more weight than was absolutely necessary.

The station had a primitive look about it; the buildings were mainly of timber with roofs of corrugated iron, and there were some sidings with a few battered trucks standing in them, abandoned, as though, having wandered in there by some mischance, they had been unable to find a way out and would in consequence be doomed to stay there for ever, quietly and gradually rusting away. There were some posters that had been desecrated by vandals, a map of the railway system of the country, and a few wooden benches for the benefit of waiting passengers. On one of the benches a man was stretched out, fast asleep, undisturbed even by the arrival of the train; he looked no more likely to be going anywhere than the abandoned trucks.

Some twenty or thirty people got off the train with Blade and drifted away. He drifted with them. Outside the station there was a taxi — an old and ill-treated Buick. A man was dozing behind the wheel, exhibiting no apparent desire for custom. Blade walked across to the car and spoke through the open window.

'Can you take me to the Hotel Segovia?'

The man gave a start and blinked at him with sleepy eyes. He had untidy black hair and his appearance would have been improved by a shave; a pungent odour of sweat, tobacco and bad breath flowed from him in sufficient volume to persuade Blade not to approach any closer.

'Señor?'

Blade patiently repeated the question and this time it appeared to sink in; the man admitted, though without enthusiasm, that he could indeed take Blade to the Hotel Segovia.

'If that is your wish, señor.'

He seemed to be giving Blade the opportunity to change his mind, to abandon the whole idea and go away, leaving him to continue dozing undisturbed. Blade had no intention of doing so; he opened the rear door of the Buick, tossed his bag on to the seat, followed it in and slammed the door behind him. The driver gave a sigh of resignation and started the engine.

It was not a long journey. Quintuaquintzl was a sprawling town but not a very large one, and there was an impression of somnolence about it which matched the sleepiness of the taximan; it could have been the effect of the afternoon heat. There was also a similar impression to that given by the railway station, a sense of everything having slipped back in time; Blade had a feeling that horsemen might ride in, dusty and sweating, from the ranges beyond the limits of the town, that mule-wagons might come rattling along the street or gold prospectors suddenly appear with laden donkeys. But it was no more than a fancy; there were no horses, no mules, no donkeys; only a sprinkling of cars and lorries, for the most part as old and battered as the taxi in which he himself was travelling.

The Hotel Segovia was near the centre of the town, a dirty white building three storeys high, standing back from the road behind an unpaved forecourt. The taxi came to a halt on the forecourt and Blade got out, taking the bag with him. He paid the driver and watched him drive away; then he walked to the hotel entrance and went inside.

It was cooler within, away from the torrid glare of the sun, and it was as still and silent as an empty cave. There was a bare tiled floor and on the left was a reception desk with a pair of feet resting on it. There were socks on the feet but no shoes, and when Blade had advanced to the desk he saw that the feet belonged to a man who was asleep in a chair on the other side. Sleep appeared to be a favourite pastime in Quintuaquintzl.

There was a bell on the desk. Blade gave it a thump with the heel of his hand and the man's head jerked up and his eyes opened. He saw Blade looking at him and he slid his feet off the desk and stood up.

'Señor?'

'I want a room,' Blade said.

The man, who was presumably the reception clerk, was middle-aged, plump and sagging, with a thin moustache and bulbous eyes; a rather seedy-looking character who matched the general aspect of the hotel. He stared at Blade, glanced down at the travel-worn bag, and seemed favourably impressed by neither.

'A single room, señor?'

'Yes.'

The clerk appeared to suppress with some difficulty an outbreak of wind. He opened the hotel register and pushed it towards Blade.

'You will please sign, señor.'

Blade did so. The clerk turned the register and examined the entry.

'You are English, señor?'

'Yes.'

'You have a passport?'

'Naturally.'

'May I see it?'

'Why?'

The clerk shrugged. 'Regulations. A formality.'

Blade produced his passport. The clerk gave it a cursory inspection, then handed it back.

'Satisfactory?' Blade asked.

'Perfectly, señor.'

'So now perhaps, the room?'

'The room, yes.' The clerk took a key from a rack behind him, turned and again faced Blade. 'You will be staying how long, señor?'

'A day, two days, possibly longer.'

'You have not yet made up your mind?'

'No.'

'And you are here on business? Or pleasure perhaps?'

Blade found it difficult to imagine that anyone would visit Quintuaquintzl on pleasure, but possibly there were such eccentrics. In any case he saw no reason why it should be any concern of a hotel clerk. He gave an ambiguous answer of which the man could make what he would.

'Perhaps.'

The clerk put on his shoes, lifted the flap and came out from behind the desk.

'This way, Señor Blade.'

Since no porter seemed to be available and the clerk showed no inclination to carry the bag, Blade picked it up himself and fell in behind the other man. They went up a staircase to the first floor and along a passage to a door marked with the number '12'. The clerk opened the door and handed the key to Blade. The room was much as he had expected; far from luxurious and bearing the evidence of use by many other impermanent occupants — greasy smudges on the walls, cigarette burns on the dressing-table, certain unidentifiable stains on the somewhat threadbare carpet. He had slept in many such rooms in the course of his life and their inherent dinginess, their mediocre furnishing and faintly repellent odour had never yet robbed him of a moment's rest.

The clerk stood watching him with an enigmatic expression on his face. He was making no attempt to sell the merits of the room; Blade could take it or leave it for all he cared.

Blade said: 'There will be someone to see me. A man named Alvarez. You will inform him that I am here when he arrives?'

The clerk gave a nod. Blade wondered whether there had been a certain reaction at the mention of the name; a faint glint in the bulbous eyes perhaps? But there was no alteration in the enigmatic expression, and why should there have been any reaction? It was probably imagination. And certainly there was nothing in the man's answer to give cause for misgiving regarding him.

'Yes, señor,' he said. 'I will inform Señor Alvarez that you are expecting him.'

He went away, closing the door softly behind him. Blade crossed to the window and looked out. Nothing of interest met his gaze; a sprinkling of traffic moving along the street, some buildings of no architectural interest on the other side, a man sleeping in the shade of a wall. He turned away from the window, kicked off his shoes and lay down on the bed, waiting for Señor Alvarez.

He fell asleep and woke two hours later, dry-mouthed and bleary-eyed, to the consciousness of the dingy room and the job still to be done. Apparently Alvarez had not yet arrived; it was perhaps hardly to be expected that he would turn up quite so quickly. The arrangement was one with which Blade was not greatly in love; he had no way of getting in touch with Alvarez; he had been given no address, no telephone number, nothing. It was entirely up to Alvarez to get in touch with him; he was to wait at the Hotel Segovia with what patience he could muster until the other man put in an appearance. And when would that be? Today? Tomorrow? Next week? There was no telling. It was a hell of an arrangement.

He lay there staring at the ceiling and thinking about it. Was he supposed to wait in the Hotel Segovia until Alvarez came? Presumably so. Well, that was going to be just fine if it turned out to be any length of time. He ought to have insisted on some other arrangement; he should have told Korvan that this was no way to do things and that he wanted to be able to get through to Alvarez as soon as he arrived in Quintuaquintzl. But he knew that he would have been wasting his breath, because obviously this was the way the customer wanted it to be, and it was the customer who was paying the piper and calling the tune. If he didn't like the tune he should never have got himself involved; it was too late to pull out now even if he wanted to. And with that ten thousand pounds dangling in front of him he had no real inclination to do so. Nevertheless, he hoped Alvarez would not be too long in showing his face.

But evening came and the face had not yet been shown. Blade ate a solitary dinner and ran his eye over the other guests. There were not many, and none of them looked like his man. Not that he had any knowledge of what his man did look like. For some reason or other he had a picture in his mind of a shifty-eyed individual, sharp-featured and hollow-chested, with a secretive manner; but there was no factual basis for this mental image; Alvarez in the flesh might be completely different, and probably was.

Blade finished his meal and moved to the lounge bar, which turned out to be as shabby as the rest of the hotel and was impregnated with a pretty strong odour of cigar smoke. Behind the bar was a sleek young man in a white steward's jacket lazily polishing glasses and listening with a fixed smile and dull eyes to a thick-set man wearing a dark suit and horn-rimmed spectacles who was sitting on a stool and apparently telling some interminable story in a low monotone. There were a few other people in the lounge, but not Alvarez — unless he was keeping himself incognito. There were two or three couples and there were four men sitting round a table completely absorbed in some discussion which obviously concerned them and no one else. The only other person was a lean, narrow-shouldered man with a leathery face who was sitting by himself and reading a magazine. It occurred to Blade that this might be Alvarez and he gave him a long hard look, but he got nothing in return and came to the conclusion that the magazine-reader was not his man.

He resigned himself to more waiting, since there was nothing else to be done, and having no desire for an evening's drinking he kept well away from the bar and the man in the horn-rimmed spectacles who looked the type who might fasten on a stranger and launch into the history of his life if given half a chance. Which was possibly what he was relating to the glassy-eyed barman.

There was a newspaper lying on a table. Blade picked it up and sat down to read. He found the exercise rather boring to say the least; the paper had all the appearance of having been strictly censored; every story was slanted in favour of the existing government and the picture that emerged was of a contented, happy country, benevolently and democratically ruled in the best interests of all the people.

So why in such a Utopia should there be an active revolutionary movement? Surely any such thing ought to be entirely unnecessary and devoid of any popular support. But the paper, of course, gave no hint that any such movement existed; the subject was obviously taboo. With a gesture of impatience Blade folded the newspaper which was so singularly lacking in real news and threw it down on the table.

'You do not find it to your taste, señor?'

Blade glanced up and saw that his attempt to avoid the man in the horn-rimmed spectacles had been useless; the man had come to him. Blade looked at him coldly; perhaps he would see that he was not welcome and would go away.

# Final Run

Unfortunately it appeared that this was not the kind of man to be repulsed by anything as unlethal as a chilly glance.

'My name,' he said, 'is Javado — Luis Javado. You do not object if I sit here?'

Without waiting for an answer he lowered his plump buttocks on to the seat beside Blade, emitting a kind of gasping sigh as he did so, rather as a fat spaniel might have done when flopping down on a hearthrug. Blade persevered with the cold stare but knew that it was useless; Señor Javado had moved in with intent to stay.

Javado tapped the paper with a thick forefinger. 'So,' he said, repeating his original question, 'you do not find it to your taste?'

'I find it,' Blade said, 'remarkably tasteless.'

Javado nodded. 'But of course that is perhaps natural, since you are not a native of this country. To a foreigner our little local affairs must appear rather uninteresting.'

Blade gave him a somewhat keener glance. 'Why do you think I am a foreigner?'

Javado smiled. 'It is not difficult to guess. You speak the language well enough, señor, but not, if you will forgive the remark, as one who learned it as a child. There is also your physical appearance which says you were not born in this part of the world.'

'And in what part of the world would you say I was born?'

Javado half-closed one eye and pursed his lips. 'North America perhaps. But no, I don't think so, Scandinavia possibly; but again no. If I were to make a guess it would be England. Would I be correct?'

'You're very shrewd,' Blade said; and it occurred to him that maybe Javado was a bit too shrewd. 'Perhaps you can also guess my name?'

Javado shook his head. 'Ah, no, señor; that would be too much to expect. I am not a mind-reader. You will have to tell me that.'

He waited expectantly. Blade let him wait for about fifteen seconds before deciding that it would be pointless to refuse the information which Javado could obtain easily enough if he inquired at the reception desk.

'Frank Blade.'

Javado thrust out a hand which Blade felt compelled to grasp. It felt like half a pound of partly-cooked sausages, warm and a trifle greasy.

'I am pleased to make your acquaintance, Señor Blade. Permit me to buy you a drink.'

Blade declined the offer. If he let Javado buy him a drink there was no telling where it would end. 'I drink very little.'

'Perhaps you are wise,' Javado said. He patted his ample stomach. 'See what drink — and too much good food — can do for you. I myself, it has to be admitted, am far too indulgent on both accounts.' He gave another gusty sigh. 'But what is a travelling salesman to do? There is so much time to kill, so many customers to entertain.'

'So you are a salesman?'

'Hardware.'

'And trade is good?' Blade asked. Not that he gave a damn whether trade was good, bad or indifferent. It was just something to say.

Javado shrugged. 'It is a living. Not a lucrative one perhaps, but a living. And you, Señor Blade?'

'I?'

'What is your line of business?'

'By a strange coincidence,' Blade said, 'I am also in the hardware trade.'

Javado looked surprised. 'Yes, that is indeed a coincidence. I hope we are not going to tread on one another's toes.'

Blade shook his head. 'I think that is very unlikely. My hardware is of a rather specialised kind.'

'Ah!' Javado appeared to be about to ask further questions but changed his mind. He pulled a cigar-case from his pocket and offered it to Blade.

'I never smoke,' Blade said.

'You have no objection if I do?'

'No. Go ahead.'

Javado went through the ritual of lighting his cigar and then began to talk about his childhood. After a time Blade felt his eyes taking on that glazed appearance he had noticed in the eyes of the barman. When he found himself actually dozing off under the soporific effect of Javado's monotonous recital he decided to break the thing up and retire to his room.

'I've had a long day and I'm rather tired; so if you will excuse me —'

Javado seemed disappointed to see his victim slipping away, but as far as Blade was concerned he could go to hell and take his disappointment with him.

'Good night, Señor Javado.'

'Good night, Señor Blade. We will continue our conversation some other time perhaps.'

'Perhaps.'

As Blade turned to leave the lounge he noticed that the leathery-faced man who had been reading a magazine was gone. Blade had not seen him leave.

Not that it was of any significance.

## Chapter Three – Business Talk

Blade slept badly, which was unusual for him. He woke several times during the night and found difficulty in getting to sleep again. When he did eventually do so he had a succession of dreams in which the hotel reception clerk and Luis Javado and the leathery-faced man were all mixed up in bizarre and meaningless incidents. When he awoke in the morning it was with a feeling of acute depression and a considerable distaste for the Hotel Segovia in general and his own room in particular. He hoped Alvarez would have the decency to arrive without much further delay; he had no desire to be kept hanging around the place for one moment longer than was absolutely necessary.

He caught sight of Javado when he went down to breakfast. The hardware salesman had a well-filled plate in front of him and was laying in some more calories with no regard whatever for his excessive waistline. He gave Blade a big smile of welcome, and a small movement of the head might have been taken for an invitation to share his table. Blade gave a curt answering nod but made no move to accept the invitation, seating himself instead at a table as far away from Javado as possible and studiously avoiding the salesman's roving eye.

After breakfast he ran the seedy reception clerk to earth and inquired whether there had been any call from Señor Alvarez.

The clerk shook his head. 'No, señor.'

'No one has asked for me?'

'No one.' The bulbous eyes regarded Blade without expression. There was a hint of weariness in them, as though the man, like Blade, had not slept well, but that was all. Again he appeared to suppress an urge to break wind, which might have indicated a tendency to dyspepsia, and added: 'If there had been anyone I should have told you, señor, as you requested.'

Blade sensed a rebuke in the protestation; an apology might perhaps have been in order but he felt no urge to offer one. He did not like the man and guessed that the feeling was mutual.

'Well,' he said, 'when Señor Alvarez does come —'

'I will tell him you are here, of course.'

'Of course.'

'And that you are very impatient to see him.'

Blade looked into the bulbous eyes again to see whether he could detect any trace of mockery, but there was nothing.

'I don't think that will be necessary,' he said. 'Just tell him I am here; that will be enough.'

'Yes, señor.'

He went to his room and found a woman making his bed. He retreated to the lounge and tried to pass the time with a magazine. After a couple of hours had dragged tediously away he came to the conclusion that Alvarez was not going to arrive that morning and that he needed a break from the hotel because it was driving him crazy. He told the clerk that he was going out for a while and that if Señor Alvarez turned up he should be informed that Señor Blade would be back shortly.

'Yes, señor.'

When he stepped outside the sunlight was dazzling, the air hot and windless. He walked slowly, taking things easy. There was no need to hurry; he was only killing time — which he sometimes thought was the hardest thing of all to kill, much harder than a man. He had certainly known places in which the killing would have been more enjoyable than in Quintuaquintzl; before he had progressed a couple of hundred yards he had reached the conclusion that it was a hell of a town, the kind anyone would be glad to get away from. And that included Frank Blade, too true it did. But for the present he was stuck there; until Alvarez turned up he could not leave. So come on, Alvarez; for Pete's sake put a jerk in it.

He came to a square in the centre of which was the statue of a man on a horse. He went up to it and discovered that it purported to represent Hernando Cortez, and he wondered why the devil anyone should have taken the trouble to erect a monument to that hard, brave, cruel and fanatical conqueror in Quintuaquintzl of all places. And why not a statue of Montezuma also, if it came to that?

He was accosted by a beggar; there were several of them gathered at the base of the statue, which appeared to be a meeting-place for them. The man who had approached him had the sombre features and beaked nose inherited from the original inhabitants of the country, the people who had owned this land before the coming of the Conquistadores; who had built pyramids and made human sacrifices on their bloodstained altars; who had constructed golden palaces and eaten the flesh of their conquered enemies.

'Señor, for the love of Christ!'

The man had no legs; he was sitting on a low wheeled trolley which he propelled with his hands. Blade tossed him a coin and he caught it skilfully and thrust it quickly into his pocket.

'Gracias, señor. May God defend you.'

They were all coming at him now, converging on him from every direction, stretching out their hands, exhibiting their sores, their malformed limbs, their tattered garments; some with blind eyes groping towards him with the others as though sensing without sight this fountain of philanthropy from which they too might catch a drop.

Blade scattered a handful of small coins, turned and fled, sickened by this display of poverty and degradation. Behind him he could hear the beggars fighting for the money, scrabbling for it in the dust, cursing and screeching. He wondered whether it might not have been better to have given nothing; what relief could such petty largesse really provide for these unfortunate creatures? The truth was that he had thrown the money more to relieve his own conscience than for strictly charitable reasons; and it failed to do even that.

As he was hurrying away from the statue he caught a glimpse out of the corner of his eye of a man on the other side of the square. The man was tall and lean and was wearing a straw hat; he was as motionless as the stone rider on the stone horse and he seemed to be looking towards Blade with a faint smile twisting his mouth. Blade could not be certain, but he had a feeling that it was the leathery-faced man who had been sitting in the hotel lounge the previous evening. Had he perhaps been following? Blade dismissed the idea; there was no reason to suppose he had been doing anything of the kind; it was not so great a coincidence that in a town the size of Quintuaquintzl they should encounter one another by accident. He put the leathery-faced man out of his mind and walked on.

He came to a café and went inside and ordered a cup of coffee. He was sitting in a booth, sipping the coffee and idly rolling between his fingers the wrapping-paper he had taken from the cubes of sugar, when again his eye was caught by the leathery-faced man. He had not seen the man enter the café, but there he was, seated no more than a dozen feet away and also sipping a cup of coffee.

It had to be more than mere coincidence this time, and Blade could not avoid a sense of uneasiness. Why should the man be following him? Was he a tail? And if so, who was he working for? The police? It was a possibility. But if that were so, it must mean that the police were suspicious; perhaps even had information regarding the true reason for his presence in the country. Yet there was no proof of that; it was surely building too much on the evidence of this chance encounter with a certain person to conclude that that person was an agent of the police. Nevertheless, this reasoning failed entirely to reassure him.

He stared at the leathery-faced man and the leathery-faced man stared back at him expressionlessly, giving no sign of recognition. Was it possible that in fact he had no recollection of seeing him in the Hotel Segovia? Some people were unobservant, took no note of those around them; but Blade would not have said that this man was such a person; he had keen eyes, watchful and intelligent.

Blade decided to force the issue. He finished his coffee and walked across to where the leathery-faced man was sitting.

'Do you have anything to say to me?'

The leathery-faced man looked up at him. 'What should I have to say to you, señor?'

'You have been following me.'

'I, señor! Following you!'

'Do you deny it?'

The leathery-faced man made a gesture of repudiation with his hands; they were as lean and cord-like as the rest of him. He had the kind of body that looked capable of withstanding much privation, tough and durable as a rawhide thong.

'What reason would I have for doing so?'

'You were at the statue of Cortez.'

'When you were distributing alms to the beggars of Quintuaquintzl?' There was a suggestion of amusement in the tone of voice, of cynical laughter in the eyes. 'It was a mistake. Forgive me for saying so, but it was surely a mistake, señor.'

'A mistake? In what way?'

'You made yourself conspicuous. Did you really wish to do that? And to what purpose? You cannot help those miserable people with a pocketful of loose change. The problem is not so easily solved, believe me. A different approach is needed; one must go to the roots of the matter, and the roots lie deep.'

'And you think I should do that? Go to the roots?'

The man shook his head. 'Not you, señor. It is not your concern. Leave it to those whose concern it is.'

'And will they do something about it?'

'Perhaps.'

'And perhaps not. Why did you say it was a mistake to make myself conspicuous? Why should it matter?'

'I think you know the answer to that,' the man said. 'You do not need me to tell you.'

'Who are you?' Blade asked. 'Why are you interested in me?'

The leathery-faced man gave a faint smile. 'Perhaps I would be interested in anyone who came to this country for the purpose of selling hardware. Hardware, shall we say, of a specialised kind?'

Blade was startled. Had the man been talking to Luis Javado? Or was it simply that he had sharp ears and had overheard some of that conversation in the lounge of Hotel Segovia?

Again Blade said: 'Who are you?'

'Good day, señor,' the man said. He picked up his coffee-cup and began to drink.

It was a dismissal, almost contemptuous in its bluntness. Blade felt angered by this cavalier treatment, but there was nothing he could do about it; he could not demand an answer to his question. Without another word he turned away from the leathery-faced man and left the café.

*

He returned to the Hotel Segovia in time for lunch. Javado was absent; perhaps he was doing business with a customer; perhaps he had left the hotel. Alvarez apparently had still not arrived. Blade was forced to contain his impatience, but he was uneasy; the encounter with the leathery-faced man had not been reassuring, to say the least; he still did not know who the man was but he could not rid himself of the suspicion that he was some kind of police or secret government agent. It had perhaps been foolish to approach him in the café; nothing had been gained by doing so.

Damn Alvarez! Why didn't he come?

Yet it was stupid to blame Alvarez; twenty-four hours had not yet elapsed since his arrival in Quintuaquintzl and it might be a day or two before his man could get in touch; there could be all kinds of reasons for the delay. Give it time, give it time. Nevertheless, he could not rid himself of the impatience, the uneasiness. Maybe he had lost his zest for this kind of thing; maybe it was just as well it was to be the final run.

# Final Run

He went up to his room and closed the door behind him, and he knew at a glance that someone had been at his luggage: the bag had been moved; it was not in the place where he had left it. It could of course have been shifted by the woman who had made the bed, but when he opened the bag he could see that it had been searched; some other person's hands had rummaged among the contents. Well, that too could have been the woman, but he did not believe so; he felt certain it had been quite a different kind of person; someone who had observed him leaving the hotel and had taken advantage of his temporary absence. And what had that person been hoping to find? Some incriminating document? Something connected with Señor Blade's business in Quintuaquintzl? Possibly.

He closed the bag and pushed it under the bed. What did they take him for? He was far too old a hand to leave anything that might compromise him lying around in a hotel bedroom. Indeed, if it came to that, he carried nothing of the kind on his person either; if anyone searched him they would find him clean; to get any evidence against him they would need to look into his brain, because that was where it was all stored away. Well, they might do that; they might even do that.

He kicked off his shoes and lay down on the bed. He was not happy. The fact that his bag had been searched did not worry him because of anything that might have been found inside it, but the fact that someone had entered the room and carried out the search was disturbing nevertheless. It was just one more pointer to the fact that people were interested in him; and he wanted no such interest, none at all. But there was nothing he could do about it; he had to accept things as they were and be on his guard. And when Alvarez eventually did turn up he would warn him to be on his guard too. If he needed any such warning. Meanwhile a little sleep might be as good a way of passing the time as any other. He closed his eyes.

He was beginning to doze when the door opened and Luis Javado eased his flabby body into the room. He had not bothered to knock but had just turned the doorknob and slipped in. Blade regretted not having locked the door, since he was not feeling any pressing need for Javado's company at that particular moment. At no other moment either, if it came to the point. Indeed, he could think of no situation in which he might conceivably regard Javado's presence as being in the least desirable.

'I hope I am not disturbing you, Señor Blade,' Javado said.

Blade stared at him coldly. 'You are.'

Javado closed the door softly. It was obvious that he had no intention of taking the hint that he was unwelcome. Blade wondered where he had eaten lunch; he felt quite sure a man as fond of his food as Javado was would not have given the meal a miss. But it was of no importance.

'I should like to have a word with you, Señor Blade.'

'You had a word with me yesterday evening, Señor Javado.'

Javado lowered his bulky frame on to the chair and gave a sigh of relief at having taken the weight off his feet.

'That is true, but now I should like another word, if it is not asking too great a favour.'

Whether it was asking too great a favour or not, Blade could see that Javado had no intention of leaving the room until he had had his word. Resigned to this fact, he sat up and lowered his feet to the floor, but remained sitting on the bed.

'You are tired?' Javado inquired solicitously. 'You did not sleep well last night?'

'Let's skip that,' Blade said. 'I'm sure you didn't come here to ask about the quality of my sleep. That's not what you're really interested in, is it?'

Javado gave a faint smile. 'It was a friendly concern for the welfare of a fellow guest, but as you say, let us skip that subject. I have been thinking about what you told me last night'

'Yes? What did I tell you?'

'That you were in the same line of business as myself — the hardware line.'

'So?'

'You said that your particular hardware was of a rather specialised kind.'

'So?' Blade said again, watching Javado closely.

Javado wriggled his shoulders and seemed faintly embarrassed. 'So I have been wondering precisely what kind of hardware it might be.'

'Why?'

'Shall we say a natural curiosity? As one who is also in the hardware business, I can hardly avoid being interested. A mutual interest, shall we call it?'

Blade had a suspicion that Javado was hinting at something more than a parallel interest between two salesmen covering the same area. It occurred to him suddenly that perhaps Javado was Alvarez using an assumed name as a precaution, and making an approach in this somewhat devious way because he was not altogether sure of his man. It was possible; it was certainly possible. But Blade also was wary.

'I am not sure it would be professionally wise to reveal that information.'

'I see that you are a cautious man,' Javado said. It was impossible to tell whether he was disappointed or not; his voice was neutral.

'Anyway,' Blade said, 'you need have no fear that our territories will overlap, seeing that my hardware is of such a special variety.'

Javado took out a handkerchief, polished his glasses, and then carefully wiped his hands. He spoke very softly, as though fearful that someone outside the room might overhear his words.

'But suppose I were to tell you that the hardware in which I myself deal is also of a very special kind, what would you say to that?'

'I would say it was an interesting statement.'

'Just so, just so. And now don't you think it might be to our mutual advantage if we were to compare notes in order to avoid the possibility of, should we say, taking up arms against each other? Figuratively speaking, of course.'

Javado paused and gazed steadily into Blade's face, apparently in the expectation, or at least the hope, that he would now reveal all. Blade did not oblige; he was still far from sure of Javado; if the man was indeed Alvarez it was up to him to lay his cards on the table first.

After continuing to gaze at Blade in hopeful silence for a while, and finding that nothing resulted from the exercise, Javado gave another sigh and said:

'You would not, I suppose, have any samples with you?'

'No,' Blade said.

'The goods are perhaps too bulky for you to carry.'

'Perhaps.'

'Or too dangerous, possibly?'

'Possibly that also.'

'A gun might conceivably fit that description.' Javado spoke musingly, his eyes still peering into Blade's. 'Do you not agree?'

'Certainly I agree.'

The handkerchief was still in Javado's hands. He folded it carefully and put it back in his pocket. Then, as though having decided that the time had come for plain speaking, he said bluntly:

'Señor Blade, are you an arms salesman?'

Blade looked at him. So after all the hints and probings they had come to it at last: the direct question. Even now, however, he was not prepared to give a direct answer.

'Are you?' he said.

Javado shook his head slowly from side to side. 'No.'

'No?'

'Señor Blade,' Javado said, with the confidential air of a man who has decided that the time has come to put all his cards on the table, 'I have a confession to make. I have not been completely honest with you.'

Blade made an effort to appear surprised at this revelation. 'Is that so?'

Javado nodded so vigorously that the folds of flesh beneath his chin opened and closed like the bellows of a concertina. 'Yes, it is so. The fact is, I am not a salesman at all. I am more in the buying than in the selling line, if you understand me.'

'Oh, I understand you,' Blade said. 'I think I understand you very well.'

He felt quite sure now that Javado was Alvarez, and the only thing he found a little difficult to understand was why he should have made such a business of revealing the fact and coming out into the open. Even now he had not reached the point of actually stating that he was Alvarez; so perhaps, before going any further, it might be a good idea to get that particular detail straightened out.

'Señor Javado,' he said, 'am I to take it that you are —'

He got no further than that because he was interrupted by a knock on the door. Both he and Javado turned their heads in that direction. Then Javado looked at him, and Blade saw that his right hand had slipped inside his jacket on the opposite side, as though reaching into an inner pocket. Javado seemed to have stiffened and there was a suspicious look on his face.

'Are you expecting a visitor?'

'No,' Blade said.

'You are sure?' There was unmistakable suspicion in Javado's voice as well as in his eyes. Blade saw that the right hand had come out a little way and that it was gripping something that could very well have been an item of hardware of a specialised variety.

'Quite sure.'

The knock was repeated; a sharp rat-tat, indicating some impatience on the part of the knocker.

'You had better see who it is,' Javado said.

Blade got up from the bed and walked to the door without bothering to put on his shoes. He opened the door and discovered the reception clerk standing outside. The man looked past him and must have seen Javado, but he showed no surprise and no particular interest.

'I have a letter for you, Señor Blade.'

The letter was in his hand, a plain sealed envelope inscribed in block lettering with the name and nothing more. Blade took it from him.

'Where did you get this?'

'It was given to me, señor.'

'By whom?'

'A man.'

'Where is the man?'

'He has gone, señor.'

Blade wondered why the clerk had brought the letter himself instead of sending it by one of the hotel staff. Perhaps he was curious and hoped to catch a glimpse of what was in the letter. Blade had no intention of satisfying his curiosity.

'Thank you,' he said, and closed the door in the clerk's face.

Javado had relaxed; both hands were now resting on his knees, both empty. He looked at the envelope and then at Blade's face, and it was obvious that he was as intrigued by the letter as the clerk had been. But Blade was not inclined to satisfy his curiosity either. He crossed to the window, stood with his back to Javado and slit open the envelope with his finger. Inside was one sheet of paper; the message on it was written in the same block lettering as the inscription on the envelope; it was lucid but laconic.

'Come to the Café San Camilo this evening at ten. A.' Blade folded the sheet of paper, slipped it back into the envelope and put the envelope in his pocket. He turned and saw that Javado was watching him intently.

'A matter of importance, Señor Blade?'

Blade shook his head. 'No; nothing of importance.'

He could see that Javado would have liked to ask more questions; would probably in fact very much have liked to read the note. But he was certainly not going to give the man that satisfaction. Indeed, he had suddenly become very suspicious of Javado. He did not sit down again on the bed, but stood with his back to the window, keeping a wary eye on Javado and especially on Javado's plump, rather stubby hands. Finally Javado gave another long, gusty sigh, which seemed to drain all the air from his lungs, and made an attempt to get back to where they had been before the interruption.

'In that case,' he said, 'perhaps we should continue our very interesting conversation. You were about to say —?'

'Nothing.'

'Nothing! But surely —'

'No, Señor Javado,' Blade said; 'I don't think we have anything more to talk about. Not anything at all.'

## Chapter Four – A Man Called Alvarez

Blade found the Café San Camilo without much difficulty. It was tucked away in a steep narrow street in one of the more squalid parts of the town where the lighting was poor and the wary pedestrian kept as far away as possible from darkened doorways.

The Café San Camilo was pretty squalid too, and the clientele seemed to be a good match for it. It occurred to Blade that if he had been looking for an assassin to do a job for him he could hardly have come to a more likely place. It was not very big and the ceiling was so low that he could easily have touched it with his hand. On the right was a small bar or counter behind which was a stout greasy-haired man in a greasy white apron who was dealing with orders, assisted by a black-haired, dark-complexioned woman with a mole on the upper lip, possibly his wife. There was a radio pumping out music in strident opposition to the various conversations that were going on, and there were a couple of electric fans doing their best to produce some movement in the hot, polluted air.

Blade cast a rapid glance round the room in search of any man who might possibly have been Alvarez, but he could see no one who appeared to fit the part; though, if it came to that, he still had not the faintest idea of what the fellow looked like and it was still up to Alvarez to make the first move.

He walked to the bar, ordered a beer and took it to a vacant table on the other side of the room. The beer was thin and frothy, but cold. He drank it slowly, watching for Alvarez and not knowing how long he would have to wait; having no desire to buy a second drink and determined to make this one last out. He was wearing an open-necked shirt and a gabardine windcheater, sufficiently grimy to pass without comment in that company, and nobody seemed to be taking any notice of him. It was not particularly flattering to reflect that he merged so well with the local scenery, but at least it was reassuring.

He had drunk about half the beer when he felt a touch on his shoulder. He turned and saw that the stout man in the greasy apron had emerged from behind the bar and had approached him from behind. Blade looked at him inquiringly. The man had a lot of dark stubble on his jowl and beads of sweat on his upper lip; at a quick estimation Blade would have rated him as being about as trustworthy as a starving hyena, but he could have been wrong; people were not always what they seemed.

The man bent down in order to bring his mouth close to Blade's left ear and spoke in a hoarse whisper, liberally spiced with the flavour of tobacco, garlic and dental decay.

'Follow me, señor.'

It was not the kind of invitation that Blade would normally have found particularly attractive, and he might have made an inquiry as to precisely whither he was expected to follow the man. But in the prevailing circumstances he decided not to ask questions, since it appeared highly probable that Alvarez would be at the other end of the line. He stood up at once, therefore, left the half-finished glass of beer on the table, and followed his bulky guide out through a doorway which opened into a rather gloomy passage with a rough brick floor.

At one end of the passage there was a wooden staircase leading to the upper regions of the establishment, and this the man began to ascend, breathing heavily from the exertion and causing the stairs to creak protestingly under his weight. Blade stayed close at his heels and hoped that the staircase would not give way beneath them. They reached the landing safely, and by the light of one dim bulb in the ceiling Blade could see a number of doors, much scratched and stained from years of faithful service.

The man in the greasy apron advanced to one of these doors and rapped on it with his knuckles. Almost immediately there was the sound of a key turning in the lock, and then the door opened — a few inches at first, then wider.

Suddenly Blade felt the hand of his guide fasten on his arm with surprising strength and before he could begin to make any resistance he was thrust bodily into the room on the other side of the door. At once the man on the inside closed the door again and locked it. He turned then and said:

'I am glad you got here safely, Señor Blade. I hope you were not followed.'

The light in the room, like that on the landing, was poor, but it was not too poor to allow Blade to recognise the speaker. It was the leathery-faced man whom he had first seen in the lounge of the Hotel Segovia and with whom he had spoken in the café not far from the statue of Hernando Cortez.

Blade stared at him. 'You!'

The man smiled faintly. 'You are surprised? You were not expecting to see me?'

'No.'

'Perhaps you were expecting to see a man called Alvarez. Is that so?'

Blade said nothing. It looked like a trap, and he had walked into it as innocently as a child. He blamed himself for having been so easily duped; a man of his experience ought to have taken precautions. Not that, even now, he could see just what precautions he could have taken; he had been working too much in the dark.

But again the other man gave his faint smile, which was the merest downward twist of the thin lips. 'Now,' he said, 'you are beginning to think you have been misled, that you have perhaps been lured into a net. Am I right?'

Still Blade said nothing.

This time the leathery-faced man gave a short laugh and clapped Blade on the shoulder. 'Don't worry. Everything is in order. I am Alvarez.'

Blade was not entirely convinced; he still had a suspicion of treachery. 'You expect me to believe that?'

'Why not? It is the truth.'

'So why did the hotel clerk tell me you had not arrived? You were already in the hotel. I saw you.'

The man who called himself Alvarez gave a lift of the shoulders, the ghost of a shrug. 'One takes precautions. The clerk did not know me by this name. It would perhaps have been wiser if you had not mentioned it either; there was no need. I would have contacted you as arranged.'

'I was led to believe that was the way it was arranged.'

'Well, perhaps; but you must understand that one has to tread very carefully.'

'I understand little,' Blade said. 'Why did you follow me this morning? Why didn't you tell me who you were when I spoke to you?'

'Because I wished to be sure of you. I had to take a close look at you first. A man who takes too much on trust doesn't live very long in this kind of business.'

'But now you're satisfied that I'm the genuine article?'

'I expect to be satisfied before you leave this room — one way or another.'

Blade got the distinct impression of a thinly veiled threat. If Alvarez failed to be satisfied he had a nasty feeling that he might not leave the Café San Camilo alive. He hoped Alvarez would be satisfied.

'All right,' he said; 'so that's settled.' He had already come to the conclusion that the leathery-faced man was indeed Alvarez. 'So what happens now?' He glanced round the room, which was lighted by one naked bulb hanging on a length of flex. There was a rough curtain covering the window and some of the plaster had fallen out of the ceiling. An iron bed pushed up against one wall had some coarse grey blankets on it, and there was practically no other furniture of any kind; even the floor was bare, the boards uneven and worm-eaten in places. 'Do we get down to talking business?'

Alvarez shook his head. 'I am not here to talk business with you, Señor Blade. That is not for me.'

Blade stared at him. 'Then what the devil are you here for?'

'To be your guide.'

'My guide!'

'You have some way yet to go. Surely you didn't think this was the end of your journey.'

'No,' Blade said, with a kind of disgust; 'I didn't really think so; it would have been too much to expect; things are never as simple as that. So now perhaps you'd better tell me all about it.'

But before Alvarez could even begin to speak there was an interruption: someone on the outside turned the doorknob and applied sufficient pressure to make the door creak slightly; but it was held by the lock and did not open.

Blade and Alvarez looked at each other, but neither spoke nor moved. The doorknob was released and returned to its normal position with a slight rattling sound. A moment later there was a gentle rap of knuckles on the upper part of the door.

Alvarez put his lips close to Blade's ear and whispered: 'Ask who it is.'

Blade did as instructed, and a muffled voice answered through the woodwork.

'A friend.'

'What do you want?'

'To speak with you.'

Again Alvarez whispered in Blade's ear. 'Unlock the door and stand aside.'

Blade once more carried out instructions; he went up to the door, turned the key in the lock and stepped away to the left. Alvarez meanwhile had backed stealthily up to the wall on the hinged side of the door. The knob again turned with that slight rattling sound and the door was pushed cautiously open to reveal the plump figure of Luis Javado standing in the opening.

He was neither fully inside the room nor fully out of it; he was halted in the halfway position, as though undecided whether to advance or retreat. But Blade did not think he would retreat; having come so far, he was hardly likely to go away again without doing whatever it was he had come to do. And what made it even more unlikely that he would go away was the fact that in his right hand he was gripping a snub-nosed revolver; because when a man went visiting with a gun in his hand it indicated that he really meant business and was not there simply to pass the time of day.

It was the revolver that caught Blade's eye and riveted his attention; it gave the lie to what Javado had said through the door about being a friend, for what kind of a friend was it who would hold a revolver pointing in the general direction of your stomach while he talked to you, as though he might have had it in his mind to put a bullet just where it could be expected to do the least good to your digestion?

'What do you want?' Blade asked again; and he wondered whether this was not rather a naïve question, since it looked only too likely that what Javado wanted was his life. 'Why are you carrying that gun?'

'Protection,' Javado said. 'There are a lot of unsavoury characters in this quarter of the town and one must look to one's safety.' He cast a quick glance to his left, as though trying to see past the hinges of the door. 'Are you alone?'

'Yes,' Blade said, without pausing to think. He wondered how Javado had managed to find him. Perhaps the man had tailed him to the Café San Camilo; perhaps he had had experience in that kind of work and was an expert. And had he come in by the front entrance and through the café? Blade doubted it; more likely that he had sneaked in by the back way without being seen. Perhaps he had been waiting in the shadows when Blade and the man in the apron had climbed the stairs.

'You are waiting for someone?' Javado inquired. 'You have an assignation maybe?'

'Is that any of your business? I imagine I may do as I please without asking your permission.'

'Oh, undoubtedly. And as to business, perhaps that is the purpose of your visit to this place? You are here to meet a customer? A buyer for some of that rather special hardware? No?'

Javado was still attempting with quick searching glances to peer into all parts of the room without taking his attention off Blade for more than a moment. It was evident that he had a suspicion that there might be another person in there, but he could not be certain of it. He was wary of moving further in, but he would eventually have to make a move of some sort, that was certain. Blade could see that he was sweating; it could have been because he was feeling the heat in that close, confined space, or it could have been because he was nervous.

'Why should I tell you who I'm meeting here?' Blade said. 'Or whether I'm meeting anyone at all, if it comes to that. Why are you so interested in my activities?'

Javado did not answer the question. He turned his head slightly and appeared to be listening. Blade also heard what had caught Javado's ear: it was the sound of someone coming up the stairs. For a moment Javado seemed undetermined what to do, and Blade guessed that he must have been wondering whether the person climbing the stairs was coming to keep the appointment in which he was so interested. But the hesitation did indeed last no more than a moment; then he stepped forward into the room and pushed the door shut with his left hand.

It was what Alvarez had been waiting for and he did not hesitate. The knife was already in his hand, though Blade had not seen it until the instant when it was used. Javado must have heard the faint sound of Alvarez moving into position, or perhaps he caught a glimpse of the other man out of the corner of his eye, for he took his attention off Blade and started to turn to the left, sensing that that was where the immediate danger lay. But he did not complete the turn because Alvarez lunged with the knife and it went in deep, went into Javado's left side just below the ribs, slanting upward and driven hard, driven in up to the hilt.

Javado made a kind of choking sound, as though there were a blockage in his throat, but that was all, no scream, no cry; and then his legs began to fold like those of a drunken man. He started to fall forward and Alvarez caught him as the revolver slipped from his fingers. Alvarez dragged him to one side and lowered him to the floor, and Javado was twitching a little, but he was not really trying to get up; he was not trying to do anything, and indeed would never try again, never.

Alvarez straightened up, and he was breathing a shade rapidly; it might have been from the brief, sudden encounter or from excitement; though he appeared utterly calm and his voice was even.

'Lock the door,' he said.

Blade crossed to the door and turned the key. He could hear the sound of footsteps on the landing, but they went past without a check and the sound faded away. He turned and looked down at the body on the floor, and then at Alvarez.

'You've killed him.'

'Yes,' Alvarez said.

'Why? Was it necessary?'

Alvarez stooped and picked up the revolver. 'There was this. Would you have wished him to use it?'

'You could have taken it from him.'

'Perhaps. And perhaps he would have killed me as I was trying to do so. It was not a chance I felt inclined to take. Besides, as long as he was alive he would have been a danger. He is better dead; all these government agents, these police spies, are no better than vermin and deserve to be exterminated.'

'How do you know he was a government agent?'

'What else could he be? What else did you imagine he was?'

'For a time,' Blade said, 'I thought he was you.'

Alvarez looked startled. 'I!'

'I had not been told what Alvarez looked like. This man approached me, throwing out hints. What was I to think?'

'And he knew why you were here?'

'I'm not sure he knew for certain; but there's no doubt he had suspicions. Pretty strong suspicions.'

Alvarez glanced down at the dead Javado. There was a dark stain round the handle of the knife and some blood had dripped on to the floor. Alvarez stirred the body contemptuously with his foot.

'Much good his suspicions did him. He would have been wiser to keep his nose out of this affair.'

'And what do we do now?' Blade asked. He could see trouble lying on the floor, bad trouble, a dead body on their hands. A body of any kind would have been bad enough; the body of a government agent was as bad as anything could be. It was a mess; he had not been in the country a week and already it was one big stinking mess. 'What in hell do we do now?'

'Now,' Alvarez said, 'we proceed with our business.'

'As if nothing had happened?' Blade pointed a finger at the body of Javado. 'What do we do about that?'

'You do nothing. I will make the necessary arrangements.' He sounded, Blade thought, like a funeral director soothing a bereaved and sorrowing relative. 'You will go back to your hotel, pack your bag and check out.'

'And then?'

'Then you will go to the Plaza Hernando Cortez where I saw you this morning. I will pick you up there.' Alvarez examined his wrist-watch. 'In two hours from now. Do you find that satisfactory?'

'I don't find anything satisfactory,' Blade said, 'but I suppose I shall have to do as you say.'

'It would be best.'

To Blade it looked as though it might turn out to be a very poor best, but he could think of no alternative that seemed any more attractive. He gave a shrug of resignation and accepted the situation.

'All right then; we'll do it your way.'

'And Señor Blade,' Alvarez said, 'when you leave the café try to look a little less concerned. People will think you have seen a ghost.'

'If it had been only a ghost,' Blade said bitterly, 'I wouldn't mind. It's the corpse that really bothers me.'

## Chapter Five – Night Drive

Back at the Hotel Segovia he went immediately to his room and packed his bag. It did not take long. He looked at his watch and saw that he still had more than an hour to spare. He reckoned that it would take no more than ten minutes, or fifteen at the most, to walk from the hotel to the Plaza Hernando Cortez, and he thought of going down to the bar and buying himself a good strong drink, but he decided not to; he had never had much faith in the kind of confidence that came out of a bottle; it was a very unreliable confidence at best and all too liable to evaporate as quickly as the stuff that produced it. Instead, he lay down on the bed and tried to relax; which in the circumstances was about as easy as relaxing on a railway line with the next train due any minute.

He found himself watching the door and imagining that Javado might walk in and start talking about hardware; but that was nonsense, because Javado was never going to walk into any more rooms and never going to talk again about hardware or anything else; he had finished with all that.

And then he got to wondering what Alvarez was doing with the body, and that was a pretty unproductive line of speculation too; so what with one thing and another, he was not at all sorry when it was time to go. He got off the bed, took his bag and the door-key, and went down to the reception desk and told the clerk he was leaving.

The man's bulbous eyes seemed to become a little more bulbous with surprise.

'You wish to leave now? Tonight?'

'That's right.'

'But why, señor? Is the room not comfortable?'

'It's comfortable enough, but I've decided to move on.'

'Nothing is wrong, I hope, señor?' The clerk was obviously curious regarding this sudden departure so late in the day. He would certainly have liked to know the reason, but Blade had no intention of telling him.

'Nothing is wrong. Just tell me what I owe and I'll pay you. Right?'

The clerk made quite a business of adding up the bill, and Blade had the impression that he was purposely wasting time over it because he was aggrieved at not having been given any explanation for the change of plan. Blade had difficulty in controlling his impatience; much more delay might mean that he would not be able to reach the Plaza Hernando Cortez at the time arranged. But the bill was at last made out. He paid it and left the hotel, aware of the clerk's gaze, curious and even perhaps a trifle suspicious, following him until he was out of sight.

He need not have feared being late; when he reached the Plaza there was no sign of Alvarez. Ten minutes went past and he had still not arrived. Blade sat on a bench under the stone eye of the great conquistador and waited. The Plaza was not particularly well lighted and there were surprisingly few people about at that hour. A jeep approached, moving slowly, and when it came closer he could see two uniformed policemen sitting in it. The one who was not driving turned his head and looked towards the bench; then he appeared to say something to the driver and Blade thought the jeep was going to stop, but it went straight on and he breathed more freely.

Five more minutes ticked away, and he was feeling pretty sore at Alvarez because there was a nasty possibility that the jeep might come back, and next time it might stop and the policemen might get out and want to know why he was waiting there with a packed bag; which was the kind of awkward question that was not going to be very easy to answer in a way that would be likely to satisfy a couple of disbelieving officers of the law.

At the end of another five minutes he was not so much sore at Alvarez as worried about him. Suppose Alvarez had run into trouble getting rid of Javado's corpse; suppose he had already been arrested. That was not at all a pleasant thought, because if the police had got hold of Alvarez, how long would it be before they got round to discovering that a certain Frank Blade was involved in the affair and decided to pick him up too?

He was getting as jumpy as a cat by this time, and when his ear caught a kind of rattling sound away to the left he swung round and stared in that direction with his pulse rate surging up as if somebody had given it a touch of the old accelerator. For a moment he wondered what the devil it was coming out of the shadows, but then he realised that it was the legless beggar on his little trolley. He had imagined that all the beggars had gone away to wherever it was they spent the night, but it was apparent now that there was at least one of them left.

The man started a whining appeal for charity even before he had reached the place where Blade was sitting. He came to a halt at Blade's feet and looked up at him in supplication, but also with a kind of defiance.

'Señor, be generous. Have pity on one less fortunate than yourself.'

'I had pity on you this morning,' Blade said.

The man looked at him more closely. 'Ah, so it is you, señor.' He cast a quick, intelligent glance at the bag. 'You are waiting for someone?'

Blade felt no obligation to answer the question, but the man was not put off by his silence.

'So we have that much in common,' he said. 'I too am waiting for someone.'

'You?'

The man gave a bitter laugh, ending on a curiously fluting note. 'I am always waiting. My whole life is spent in waiting. Some day I shall die and the waiting will be finished; I shall no longer need to beg for charity; I shall be free at last.'

'We shall all die some day,' Blade said. He felt in his pocket, took out a ten-peso note and gave it to the man, who accepted it with an inclination of the head which seemed to have in it a certain mockery.

'That is true,' he said. 'Life is brief even at the best.'

Blade thought of Javado. For some unnaturally brief. The thread could be so easily cut. It was not a cheerful thought.

The legless man seemed inclined to linger. He glanced again at the bag, as though trying to work out in his mind why Blade should be sitting there with this article of luggage. But if he was curious he was not apparently prepared to put a direct question. Blade felt uneasy under the man's unwavering gaze and wished he would go; but there seemed to be no way of making him do so if he had no wish to move on. And where in hell was Alvarez?

The car came up fast and stopped with a squeal of brakes some twenty paces away from the bench. It was a not very new convertible with one man in it. The man leaned out and beckoned with his hand. Blade could not see him very clearly but guessed that it was Alvarez. And about time, too. He got to his feet and picked up the bag.

The legless man looked up at him. 'You are leaving, señor?'

'Yes,' Blade said.

He began to walk towards the car and heard the rattle of the legless man's trolley following him. He reached the car with the beggar no more than a pace or two behind him.

The driver of the car was indeed Alvarez. 'Get in,' he said. He sounded impatient, as though it were he who had been kept waiting.

Blade opened the door, threw his bag on to the rear seat, and got in beside Alvarez.

'Adios, señor,' the beggar shouted. 'And God go with you.'

The words were fine, nothing wrong with them; but the shouted farewell had in it a jeering, vindictive note that was not quite so pleasant. It was almost as though the man had added: 'And the devil take you!'

Alvarez got the car going. He said: 'You have been talking to that man?'

'He spoke to me and I answered him,' Blade said.

'You did not tell him anything?' There was a sharpness in the question that made it sound like an accusation.

Blade resented the suggestion. 'Do you take me for a complete idiot? Do you imagine I've been telling him my business? Telling him about you? About Javado?'

'It would have been better not to have spoken to him at all. The police use these beggars as informers.'

'You should have warned me. And if I had not been made to wait so long I might not have been accosted. It's more than half an hour beyond the time you arranged to pick me up. What kept you?'

'There were difficulties.'

'In getting rid of Javado?'

'Yes.'

'But you managed it? It all worked out?'

'It all worked out,' Alvarez said. 'In the end.'

Blade's misgivings were not entirely set at rest by this reply; that remark concerning difficulties had a disquieting sound. What sort of difficulties? He thought of asking for more details, but decided not to. Later perhaps.

Alvarez was driving carefully, not speeding, taking no risks; and Blade concluded that he wished to avoid any argument with traffic police. To be pulled up for a driving offence or to be involved in a minor accident would be to attract the very attention he least desired.

Traffic was in fact rather sparse, and when they got clear of the town there was very little of it at all. Alvarez must have felt somewhat easier in his mind then; he put a bit more pressure on the accelerator and had the convertible moving at a pace that was soon piling up the kilometres between it and Quintuaquintzl.

'Would it be asking too much to inquire where we're going?' Blade said.

He saw Alvarez's head turn momentarily towards him. 'What good would it do you to know that?'

'No good at all perhaps. But I should like to know just the same, if you have no objection.'

Alvarez gave a laugh. 'Oh, I have no objection. We are heading for a town called Esperanza.'

'A hopeful name, if nothing else. And when do you hope to arrive?'

He saw Alvarez's shoulders lift. 'It is one hundred and twenty kilometres and the road is not good. We are in God's hands.'

Blade reflected that he himself was also in Alvarez's hands, and he would have preferred not to be. It was not that he did not trust the man, but Alvarez was serving a cause and to such men everything else was liable to be of secondary importance — including the life of anyone not fully committed to the same sacred endeavour.

'And when we get to Esperanza, what then?'

'You will see.'

'In other words, you don't intend to tell me?'

'It will be soon enough when we get there.'

The road stretched ahead into the night. There were glimpses of fences slipping past on either side, clumps of trees, huge piles of rocks, massively dark against the star-bright sky.

Blade was silent for a time, but his thoughts kept going back to that room above the Café San Camilo, with Javado dead on the floor. Finally he asked the question that kept coming into his head.

'How did you dispose of the body?'

'You really wish to know?' Alvarez inquired. 'It bothers you?'

'I feel a natural curiosity. After all, I am rather intimately involved.'

'And would rather not be, perhaps?'

'In that kind of business, yes. But it is done now and can't be undone.'

'Yes,' Alvarez said; 'it is done.'

'And the body?'

'Two men took it away in a truck.'

'You trust these men?'

'They are being paid. And how would it profit them to betray us? They would end up in the same state as Javado. They are well aware of that.'

'And the people at the café?'

'They are dependable. Never fear about them.'

'What will the men do with the body?'

'That is for them to decide. I did not ask. Maybe they will bury it or drop it down a crevasse. One thing you can be sure about: it will not be found.'

Blade hoped Alvarez's trust in his agents was justified, but for his own part he had doubts; he would not have put much reliance on the good faith of two men who were prepared to dispose of a dead body for pay. But perhaps, as Alvarez had hinted, the fear of going the same way as Javado would be a sufficient argument in favour of keeping a still tongue in the head.

\*

It was not yet day when they drove into Esperanza. There was a huddle of dark buildings, a broad main street running down between them, a few lights showing here and there, no one moving as far as Blade could see. It seemed like the wrong hour to arrive.

'Nobody told them we were coming,' he said. 'They haven't put the flags out.'

It was not the wittiest remark in the world, but he was not feeling very witty after a rough night in a car. He was feeling tired and dirty, dry-mouthed and faintly nauseated; not happy with himself, not happy with Alvarez, not happy with anything.

Alvarez made no pretence of being amused; he was probably feeling pretty foul too; after all, he had done the driving and had not been able to snatch even a few winks of sleep. He answered in a sour tone of voice:

'Publicity is not what we are looking for; the less attention we attract, the better it will be for both of us.'

'It was only a joke,' Blade said. 'Maybe it was a poor one at that. Forget it.'

Perhaps with the idea of attracting as little attention as possible, Alvarez was again driving very carefully, keeping the speed of the convertible down to a level that could hardly have contravened even the strictest regulations. It could have been because he was a little uncertain of the way; he kept glancing from one side to the other, as though searching for a familiar landmark; but finally he gave a grunt of satisfaction and swung the car off to the right, the beam from the headlights washing briefly over a white stone building with a colonnade, which looked rather more imposing than those surrounding it and might well have housed the administrative offices.

The road dipped steeply downhill and then levelled out, and still Alvarez was keeping the speed down, though he now seemed more certain of the way. He took a turning to the left into a narrow lane with a lot of potholes which tested the springing of the car and prompted him to reduce the speed even more; and then he gave another grunt, hauled on the wheel to make a sharp turn, and a moment later they were slipping through a gateway into a yard of some sort with a dilapidated wooden fence surrounding it.

Alvarez stopped the car and switched off the ignition and the lights.

'We're here.'

For a while neither of them made any move to get out; they just sat there as though savouring this moment of relaxation. It was all very still and quiet; nothing to break the silence but a slight cracking sound now and then from the engine as it began to cool. It had seemed very black when the lights were switched off, but as Blade's eyes became accustomed to the darkness he could make out the solid shape of a building and a tree or two outlined against the sky. There was no light showing in the house and no evidence of anyone being awake.

'They're all in bed. Maybe we got here too early.'

Alvarez stirred himself and opened the door on his side of the car. 'Come,' he said. 'Bring your bag.' He stepped out, closed the door quietly and started walking towards the house.

Blade lifted his bag off the rear seat and followed. The yard was just hard-packed earth which probably dissolved into mud when the rain came; in places tough grass had taken root, clinging tenaciously to life in adverse circumstances. Alvarez led the way to the front of the house and they came to a door. He hauled on an iron ring and there was a harsh grating sound followed by the faint tinkle of a bell inside the house. Nothing happened. They waited a while and then Alvarez gave another vigorous tug at the bell-pull, which he backed up with some lusty work on a knocker.

This did the trick; a few moments later a man's voice, gruff and suspicious, almost directly above their heads, demanded: 'Who's that? What do you want?'

They had to step back from the door to get a view of the owner of the voice; he was leaning over the iron rail of a small balcony and he was obviously a man who believed in taking no chances with people who knocked him up in the early hours of the morning, for he had a shotgun in his hands and the barrel was pointing at the two on the ground. Blade would have felt happier if it had been pointing in some other direction, preferably upward, because at that range it would have taken only a very little pressure on the trigger to make a bloody mess of both him and Alvarez.

Alvarez must have been having similar thoughts, for he said sharply: 'Put the gun away, Carlos. You know me — Alvarez. Do you wish to shoot me?'

'Ah, is it you, Señor Alvarez?' the man named Carlos said. He withdrew the gun and Blade was thankful for that. 'I did not expect you so soon.'

'Never mind what you expected,' Alvarez said; and he sounded impatient. 'Come down and open the door.'

'At once, at once.'

The man's head disappeared from sight and not long after that the sound of bolts being slipped back could be heard. The door opened, revealing Carlos with the light behind him, a bulky figure dressed in shirt and trousers hurriedly thrown on, his feet bare, his black hair in an untidy tangle.

'Enter, señores.'

He stood back to one side. Alvarez and Blade walked into the house and he closed the door behind them and bolted it.

There was no appearance of any luxury in the house; the furniture was old and plain, the drapery a trifle threadbare; there were no carpets on the floor. Yet everything was spotlessly clean and tidily arranged, giving evidence of care and even pride. The room to which Carlos conducted them had whitewashed walls and a low ceiling.

He said: 'You have come a long way and are tired no doubt. You will wish to rest.'

'We are hungry,' Alvarez said.

'Of course. My wife will prepare a meal for you. I will fetch her.'

But she was already in the room, a thin, austere woman with a firm mouth and dark hair scraped back from a high forehead. If she had dressed hurriedly there was no hint of it in her appearance, and there was no sleep in her eyes, which were shrewd and observant. Her age, Blade guessed would be something over fifty, possibly a few years short of her husband's.

Alvarez turned to her. 'Your pardon, señora, for arriving at such an hour, but it was unavoidable.'

'You are welcome in this house,' she said, 'at any hour, day or night, as I think you are aware.' Her voice was in keeping with the rest of her: thin, precise, emotionless. 'I will get the food at once.'

She was gone immediately, asking no questions, showing no surprise, no resentment at being roused from bed.

'An excellent woman,' Alvarez said, a note of genuine admiration in his voice.

Carlos agreed. 'A treasure. A man is indeed fortunate to have such a wife.'

The words were unexceptionable, but Blade thought he detected a certain lack of warmth. It was possible that Carlos, who looked an easy-going, even slovenly kind of man, found the undoubted excellence of his partner in life something of a trial. She had put a polish on the furniture and perhaps she had attempted to put a polish on him. If so, she had from all appearances been rather less than successful.

That she was as handy with a cooking-stove as with a duster Blade was able to judge for himself when the meal was served. It was an early breakfast but he was hungry enough to do justice to it, as Alvarez was also. Carlos went away to complete his toilet while the woman stayed on hand, answering briefly when Alvarez spoke to her but making no effort to keep a conversation going.

After the meal Blade went to sleep in an armchair and was unaware of anything more until he awoke suddenly to find the woman grasping his shoulder in one skinny hand and shaking him vigorously. It was broad daylight and through the window he could see the sun shining brilliantly. He sat up and the woman stopped shaking him and released his shoulder.

'Ah,' she said, 'so you are awake now.'

'I'm awake,' Blade said. 'What's going on? Where is Señor Alvarez?'

The woman stood with her hands clasped in front of her, looking primly down at him. There was no sign of Carlos, her husband.

'Señor Alvarez is gone,' she said.

Blade sat up. 'Gone? Gone where?'

'I cannot tell you. I was not told.'

'But when will he be back?'

'He is not coming back.'

It sounded crazy; she must have got it wrong; Alvarez would not go off like that without as much as a word; it just did not make sense.

'He'll have to come back. We have unfinished business.'

She shook her head. 'No, señor. Your business, I think, is now with someone else.'

A man's voice broke in then: 'With me, Señor Blade, if you do not mind.'

It was a gentle, good-humoured voice. Blade glanced towards the door and saw a short, round, plump man in a threadbare and somewhat greasy black cassock. He was almost completely bald, with no more than an untidy fringe of hair at the base of his scalp; yet his brown, chubby face and sparkling eyes gave him an oddly youthful look. He was wearing a pair of leather sandals but no socks, and his feet were grimy. There was a good deal of grime on his hands also.

'Allow me to introduce myself,' he said. 'I am Father Rubello. You are to come with me now. If you are ready we will leave at once. I have a car.'

## Chapter Six – Surprise From Father Rubello

It was a white Volkswagen Beetle and it looked as if it had taken quite a hammering in the line of duty; there were dents in the wings and that famous Volkswagen paintwork had been chipped all the way down through the layers to the metallic bedrock in places. Blade wondered whether Father Rubello drove like the devil himself or whether the car had been in this condition before falling into his hands. Certainly he did not look like a man who could afford to buy a new car; but if it came to that, it would have been difficult for any man to appear affluent in a greasy cassock and scuffed sandals.

The house looked smaller than it had seemed to be in the darkness, as though it had shrunk into itself with the approach of day. The sunlight revealed the decay that had set in, the cracked stucco and the peeling paint. The woman stood in the doorway with her hands clasped in front of her in that way she had and watched them leaving. From the expression on her face, severe, unsmiling, it was impossible to tell whether she was glad to be rid of them or not. Blade had not had time to get to know her; he was not sure that he wanted to; he had a feeling that she despised him, but no firm evidence that she did.

He slung his bag into the back of the Volkswagen and eased himself on to the front seat. Father Rubello got in behind the wheel and seemed to have some difficulty in reaching the pedals with his feet. He waved a hand out of the window in farewell.

'Adios, señora. May God keep you.'

The woman made no answer and did not wave back. Father Rubello started the engine and shifted the gear lever. The Beetle began to move, bouncing over the potholes. As they left the yard Blade glanced over his shoulder and saw the woman still standing in the doorway of the house with her hands clasped and her face rigid. He wondered where her husband was. Maybe he had gone away with Alvarez — wherever Alvarez had gone.

Esperanza had come to life; it was no longer a dark, silent collection of buildings momentarily revealed by the headlamps of Alvarez's car, as it had been when Blade had first seen it; now the houses were clearly visible in the hard sunlight and people were going about their business. A market had sprung up in an open square; there were goods set out for display on the bare ground; woven mats, coloured blankets, earthenware, fruit and vegetables in great variety. Women dressed in sombre black sat patiently waiting for custom. A bus, so old that it would have been a museum piece in a richer country, clattered to a halt and discharged its load of humanity. There was an impression of dust and sweat and poverty.

'This is your first time in Esperanza?' Father Rubella inquired, like a man making polite conversation.

'Yes,' Blade said. He refrained from adding that he hoped it would also be his last, since it might possibly be Father Rubello's home town and people were inclined to be sensitive on the subject of home towns.

The little priest drove with care, his short, plump fingers gripping the steering-wheel as though it might have been a cup of sacramental wine from which not a drop must be allowed to spill. The engine of the Volkswagen was perhaps in better condition than the bodywork; certainly it appeared to be running well enough. When they were clear of the town Father Rubello seemed to relax; the road was bad but traffic was light.

'How far do we have to go?' Blade asked.

'Eighty kilometres. Perhaps a little more. It would be much less in a direct line, but unfortunately the road does not run straight.'

He did not exaggerate in that respect; the road was serpentine in its twists and turns, forced into these contortions by the mountainous character of the landscape. It was barren country with few signs of habitation, harsh and sun-baked and inhospitable.

Blade wondered whether Father Rubello had been told of what had happened in Quintuaquintzl, and if so whether it troubled his conscience at all. Perhaps he accepted the necessity for such violence in the cause which he apparently served just as Alvarez did. He caught a sidelong glance from the priest's twinkling eyes.

'You are thinking perhaps that it is strange for a man of God to be involved in this kind of enterprise?'

Blade admitted that the thought had indeed crossed his mind.

'Yet it is not so strange,' Father Rubello said. 'Anyone who has the good of the people at heart must do what he can to help overthrow the forces of oppression.'

'Even by violent means?'

'The Roman Catholic Church has never recoiled from violence when violence has been necessary in a holy cause.'

'And this is a holy cause?'

'That surely cannot be doubted.'

'You are taking a great risk, Father.'

'All life is a risk; and what have we to lose but life itself? Which is no true loss, since it is the key to something infinitely finer, infinitely more desirable.'

'If one believes.'

'And you do not?'

'I believe in this life. I have seen no proof of any other.'

'And you demand proof — as Thomas did?'

'I am not a man to take anything on trust.'

Father Rubello chuckled softly. 'You are taking me on trust. What proof have you that I am what I appear to be? Did Alvarez vouch for me?'

Blade had to admit that Alvarez had not even mentioned Father Rubello.

'Yet you came with me without question.'

'What alternative was there?'

'You could have refused.'

'And gone back home with nothing accomplished! What profit would there be in that?'

The priest nodded. 'And you, of course, are in this solely for profit.'

'Did you imagine I would have any other motive?'

'So you are willing to risk your life for money?'

'You think my life is at risk?'

Father Rubello smiled. 'I don't think you are foolish enough, Señor Blade, to have any doubts of that. There are people who would not wish you to succeed in what you have come here to do; people who would stop at nothing to prevent you from completing your business. I am sure you are very well aware of that.'

Blade thought of Luis Javado and could not deny the truth of what Father Rubello had said.

'This is a violent country,' Father Rubello continued. 'It has always been so — even before the Spanish came. Some day we shall have peace; but first there will be much fighting, much bloodshed, much suffering; that is certain.'

Blade hoped he would be well out of it before the fighting started; he was not keen to be mixed up in that kind of thing.

It was about midday when Father Rubello took the car off the road and brought it to a halt in the shadow of a clump of trees.

'It is time for a little refreshment, don't you think?'

Blade looked about him. It was a wild spot, scenically impressive, but deserted.

'Refreshment! Here?'

Father Rubello's brown eyes twinkled. 'Oh, you will find no restaurant here; there is probably not an establishment of that description within thirty or forty kilometres. But I did not come unprepared. We shall do well enough.'

Blade saw no cause to disagree with this assessment when Father Rubello had taken a cloth-covered basket from the boot of the car and revealed its contents. There were sandwiches of roast chicken and ham, sausages, a fruit pie, cheese, some cans of beer and two bottles of white wine. The little priest spread the cloth in the welcome shade of the trees and laid out the feast with the eager anticipation of a man for whom eating was one of life's keenest pleasures.

'The beer and wine may be a trifle warm,' he said, 'but one cannot always hope for perfection.' He put his hands together, bowed his head and mumbled a few words which might have been a form of grace but were unintelligible to Blade, and then said briskly: 'Don't wait. Help yourself.'

He was already doing as much for himself, and Blade waited for no second invitation but followed suit at once.

'You certainly came well prepared, Father.'

Father Rubello laid a hand on the smooth curve of his stomach. 'Perhaps I am in mortal danger,' he said.

'Danger!'

'Of the sin of gluttony.' Father Rubello spoke with his mouth full and appeared to accept with equanimity the possibility of succumbing to number five in the list of the seven deadly sins. Possibly he calculated that there would be ample opportunity to repent and compensate with a spell of fasting before the time came for his account to be totted up.

In their position among the trees they were entirely hidden from the road. They could hear the occasional sound of a vehicle going past, but there was not much traffic and there were considerable intervals when nothing seemed to be moving. When they had finished the meal Father Rubello clasped his hands over his stomach, leaned back against the bole of a tree and closed his eyes.

'We are not pressed for time. A short rest in the interests of digestion will do neither of us any harm.'

Blade saw no reason to argue with that. The good food, the wine and the heat of the day combined to induce a feeling of drowsiness. He also closed his eyes and was almost immediately asleep.

It was a sharp pain in the left side that roused him. He opened his eyes and saw a man standing over him. There was another man a few yards away and they made an evil-looking pair. They were wearing frayed trousers and shirts and battered old straw hats under which a lot of straggling black hair was visible; they were unshaven and smelled of sweat, and their skins were darkly tanned by the sun. Blade would not have trusted them even if they had been unarmed; the long-barrelled revolvers they were carrying merely strengthened his conviction that they were not to be trusted.

The one who was standing over him, and who had apparently kicked him in the side to waken him, spoke in a harsh, growling voice which had no hint of friendliness in it.

'Get up.'

Blade got up. With a revolver pointing at him and a dirty forefinger wrapped round the trigger, it was no time to refuse an order. His lower ribs were still hurting from the effects of the kick, and he just hoped none of them were broken, because a cracked rib was one of the last things he wanted to be saddled with at that particular time and in that particular place. And if it really came to the point he never did want to be saddled with a cracked rib — any time, any place.

The man had a long, thin neck with a jumpy Adam's apple and a mouthful of bad teeth. He said:

'Have you got a gun?'

'No,' Blade said.

The man was not one to take that kind of statement at its face value; he stepped forward and ran a hand over Blade just to make sure. Blade got the full impact of the man's stench, bad breath included, and it turned his stomach. The man found no hidden weapons; he took a pace back and appeared to relax a little.

The other man was watching Father Rubello; he had a hooked nose and he breathed through his mouth. Father Rubello was standing up and his hands were lifted, palms outward in a gesture of protest at what was going on.

'My sons,' he said in a placatory tone of voice. 'What are you doing? What do you want?'

The thin-necked man gave a sneering laugh, thrust his revolver into his belt and picked up one of the wine bottles. It was half full and he drank from the bottle, spilling some of the wine so that it dribbled down his chin.

'The wine is yours, my son,' Father Rubello said. 'And if you are hungry there is food. Take what you will.'

The man passed the bottle to his companion and wiped his mouth with the back of his hand. 'We'll take what we wish, priest — by your leave or without it. Do you think you can stop us?'

'You have guns,' Father Rubello said.

'And we may use them. Remember that — priest.'

The way the thin-necked man spat out the final word seemed to indicate that he had some grudge against the priesthood; but possibly he had a grudge against all society and not merely one section in particular.

The man with the crooked nose threw away the empty bottle and belched loudly; he was still holding his revolver in his hand, which had a considerable inhibiting effect on any counter-move Blade might have had in mind. And even if neither man had been armed he realised that he would have stood little chance against the two of them, for he doubted whether he could rely on any effective assistance from Father Rubello; the priest did not give the impression of being physically equipped for a rough-and-tumble even if he had had the inclination to take part in one. For the present, therefore, it seemed advisable to do nothing. He glanced in the direction of the road. The thin-necked man noticed the glance and said jeeringly:

'You think somebody is coming to help you? You can forget that. Nobody will come. You got money?'

'Not much,' Blade said.

'We see about that. You better have money. You better make us happy or you get trouble. You understand trouble — bad trouble?'

Blade understood well enough; what the man meant was that if the take was not enough to satisfy them, they would likely compensate themselves in other ways for the disappointment — by beating up their unfortunate victims and maybe even killing them. The question was, how much money would satisfy them? And even having got the money, they might nevertheless carry out the beating-up and the killing just for the hell of it. He would not have said they were the kind of men to have any scruples

Final Run

regarding torture and murder; they had probably committed both crimes on other occasions. The fact that this time one of the victims happened to be a man of God was not likely to deter them; indeed, it might give an added zest to the entertainment.

'You give me the money now,' the thin-necked man said. 'You show me what you mean by not much. Now you empty your pockets and show me.'

'If you want it,' Blade said, 'why don't you come and get it?'

The man gave a kind of snarl, stepped forward and hit Blade with his clenched fist on the side of the jaw. Blade was staggered by the sudden blow, and in a moment the man had taken a grip on his right shoulder with one hand while with the other he began searching for the money. He had taken the invitation literally and had accepted without hesitation.

The blow of the fist had done more than merely hurt Blade; it had caused his temper to flare up, and for the moment he forgot all about that cool assessment of the situation he had previously made, that rational decision to make no move which might invite retaliation. Indeed, he forgot it so completely that as soon as the thin-necked man thrust a hand into one of his pockets he brought his right knee up hard enough to give the man a lot more agony than he had yet dished out on his own account.

The man gave a grunt of pain and started to fold in the middle, but Blade put a stop to that by grabbing him round the waist and holding him upright. He needed the thin-necked man now, because the man with the crooked nose had lost interest in Father Rubello and was advancing with his revolver and an obvious intention of using it in the worst possible manner from Blade's point of view.

The thin-necked man was still making gasping noises and not putting up much of a fight, and Blade decided to let go with his right hand and make a grab for the revolver stuck in his belt. It would have been a good enough plan if it had worked; and it did work — up to a point. He got his fingers on the butt of the gun and managed to haul it out of the belt; but he had not got a really firm grip on it and a sudden movement on the part of the thin-necked man knocked it out of his hand and it fell to the ground.

The man with the crooked nose was still advancing, but he was not hurrying it; he was wary and cautious, not taking any chances. He had his own revolver cocked and pointing, but he could not take a shot because Blade was keeping the thin-necked man as a shield between them. Unfortunately, there was a limit to what you could do in that line, and he knew that as soon as the thin-necked man had got over the effects of the knee in the crotch he was going to start struggling a lot harder, and then things would become very difficult indeed. Moreover, it could not be long before the other man succeeded in getting round to the back of him and ramming the muzzle of that long revolver into the base of his spine or some other vulnerable portion of his body; and that would be that.

The thin-necked man had started cursing, so it was a hundred to one that he was feeling better, even if he was not yet in the peak of condition. His face was close enough for Blade to get the benefit of all that foul breath as well as the foul words, but they were the least of his worries; it was the revolver he could see when he looked over the thin-necked man's shoulder that really bothered him. The thin-necked man was becoming more of a handful now, so Blade gave him the knee again and that cooled him. Once again he tried to fold and Blade had to hold him upright; but it was all becoming pretty tiring, to say the least.

And then the man with the crooked nose made a sudden darting move and succeeded in getting behind him. He tried to swing the thin-necked man round to guard himself, but in doing so he tripped and they both went down.

He hit the ground with his left shoulder and it really jarred him; it jarred his neck and his head as well, and for a moment he lost sight of the man with the crooked nose. Then he heard a croaking sort of laugh and there was the nose just above him, and the revolver too, with the hammer cocked and all ready to go.

There was nothing more he could do about it now, so he just lay still and waited for the crooked-nosed man to press the trigger; hoping he would not make a mess of it and just do something horrible like blowing half his jaw away, but afraid the bastard might do that kind of thing merely for the fun of it, merely to see the victim squirm.

The man seemed to be taking a hell of a time to make up his mind about doing it, and Blade felt like yelling at him to get it over and done with. But maybe it was not really as long as all that; maybe it just seemed like it; maybe when you were waiting for a bullet to come smashing into your skull it always did seem a long time, even if it was in reality no more than a couple of seconds.

And then something else happened; something totally unexpected; something so astounding that he could hardly believe his hearing had not gone on the blink.

Father Rubello said: 'Drop the revolver or I'll shoot you dead.'

And Father Rubello's voice had altered; there was no trace of softness or gentleness in it any more; it was hard and steely, so that anyone hearing it had to believe he meant precisely what he said and was not playing games; oh, most certainly not playing games.

Blade saw the revolver that had been aimed at his head move away to the right as the crooked-nosed man began to turn; and then there was the little cracking sound of a pistol shot, and some earth and stones spurted up an inch or so from the crooked-nosed man's feet. There was the shrill whine of a ricochet too, as the bullet skidded off the rocky ground and went away on its travels.

'Next time the heart,' Father Rubello said. 'Drop it.'

The crooked-nosed man dropped it.

'Pick up the guns, Señor Blade,' Father Rubello said.

He was standing some five paces away and there was a black automatic pistol in his right hand, but at that range it was big enough. It must have been hidden somewhere under Father Rubello's cassock; which just proved that when you frisked people for guns it was wise to frisk everybody — priests included.

Blade got to his feet, scooped up the two revolvers and stepped away from the bandits. The thin-necked man was still sitting on the ground with his knees drawn up to his chest. He had a venomous expression on his face, but it was going to take a lot more than that to bother Father Rubello. The man with the crooked nose was standing with his shoulders hunched, looking sullen and crestfallen. Things had suddenly gone very wrong for the pair of them.

'What shall we do with them, Señor Blade?' Father Rubello said. 'Shall we take them along and hand them over to the police?'

Blade felt quite sure it was not a serious suggestion. Father Rubello would have no desire to get involved with the law. But the two men were not to know that.

'Or shall we simply shoot them?' Father Rubello continued musingly, as though going over the alternatives. 'It would save a lot of trouble and rid the world of a pair of worthless rascals.' He rubbed his smooth, plump chin reflectively with his left hand while the pistol dangled in his right.

The sullen look on the face of the crooked-nosed man changed to one of terror. 'No, Father! For the love of God, no!'

Father Rubello stared at him coldly. 'What better do you deserve?'

The man went down on his knees in supplication. 'Father, we are poor unfortunate men driven to do these things to live. Have mercy.'

The thin-necked man spat suddenly in disgust. 'Don't beg.' He stood up and stared at Father Rubello with malevolence but without fear. 'Shoot us then, priest. Shoot us, holy man. We are scum, not fit to live.' He spoke sneeringly. 'Do your duty to mankind. Rid the world of two parasites.' He tore his ragged shirt open, baring his hairy chest. 'Shoot and to hell with you!'

Father Rubello lifted the pistol with slow deliberation and took careful aim. The man with the crooked nose grovelled on his knees.

'No, Father, no!'

The thin-necked man turned and kicked him.

Father Rubello lowered the pistol. 'But why should I do the work of the executioner? Be off with you, you dogs. Go before I change my mind.'

The crooked-nosed man got up from his knees; he seemed hardly able to believe his good fortune.

'Bless you, Father, bless you!'

Father Rubello made an impatient gesture with the pistol. 'Go.'

The man turned and shambled off. The thin-necked man spat again, gave a shrug of the shoulders and followed him.

## Chapter Seven – Of A Sort

'You never had any intention of shooting them,' Blade said.
'It was all bluff.'

Father Rubello turned his head for a moment and smiled before concentrating again on the road ahead.

'You think so?'

'Yes.'

'So when I aimed the pistol you didn't believe I would fire it at the man's chest?'

'If I had thought you had any intention of doing so I should have tried to stop you.'

'So you are squeamish when it comes to the point,' Father Rubello said. 'You do not care for bloodshed. That is interesting; it reveals a kind of double standard; you do not object to the trade, but you must not be involved in the consequences of it. Some people might well call that hypocrisy.'

'And you. Don't you too have a double standard? A man of God who carries a gun.'

'It is hardly without precedent,' Father Rubello replied urbanely. 'Bishops have been known to lead armies. And there are, as you have witnessed, occasions when a gun, employed with discretion, may do much good. If I had not been armed those men would certainly have robbed us, if nothing worse. At least, they would have robbed you, for I have nothing.'

'You have a car.'

'True. And they might have taken it — always supposing either of them were capable of driving it. So you see, my pistol served the admirable purpose of saving those men from their own evil instincts. Indeed, if I had not had it they might even have killed us.'

'That possibility occurred to me. Don't imagine I'm criticising you; far from it. I'm only too thankful you did have a gun. It was fortunate your man didn't search you. I wonder why he didn't.'

'Because of my clothes. When a man has been born into the Roman Catholic faith, even though he may later become the most abandoned of villains, he seldom manages entirely to shake off his awe of the Church. It is something engraved on his mind, his soul.'

'You mean he remains for ever superstitious?'

'You may call it that if you wish; it is not, of course, the word I should use. Anyway, you should be glad of that superstition if it is what prevented the man from searching me.'

'I am, certainly I am. And incidentally, you seem to handle the pistol very expertly. You must have had a deal of practice.'

'It would be stupid for a man to carry a gun and not know how to use it effectively,' Father Rubello said. 'And as to whether or not I had any intention of killing the men, one thing at least is certain — the fellow who bared his chest and defiantly invited me to shoot certainly did not believe I would do it.'

'You think not?'

'I am certain of it. That is why he was so valiant. The other man believed I would do it, and so he became abject. The one had a certain rough dignity; the other had none. But the difference between them was entirely in their assessment of what I would do. Basically, I imagine, there was little to choose between the courage of one or the other.'

Blade was not sure that he entirely agreed with Father Rubello, but he was not prepared to argue the point. The main thing was that a situation which had looked like being very sticky indeed had finally turned out as well as it had. He still had a slight pain in the side and a mildly aching jaw, but neither was anything to worry about; it could have been worse, far worse.

Father Rubello had suggested keeping the revolvers, but he had disagreed with that.

'Why not?' Father Rubello had said. 'You have seen how useful a gun can be in pulling you out of trouble.'

'A gun could also get me into trouble. I've never yet carried one around with me and I don't think I'll start the habit now.'

Father Rubello had appeared faintly surprised at this but had said no more. Blade had unloaded the revolvers and thrown them away. The bandits might return later and find them, but he was not bothered about that; he did not expect to meet the men again.

They drove on in silence for a time and were soon coming to lower, less barren parts. Some of the land was under cultivation; here and there was a huddle of poor buildings or even a small village.

'When do you expect to get there?' Blade asked.

Father Rubello did not glance at him. 'Get where?'

'Wherever it is we're going.'

'We could be there in an hour perhaps, but I think we will wait until nightfall. It might be better.'

He pulled the car off the road soon after that. There was a small stream nearby; he walked over to it and began to bathe his face and hands in the clear water. Blade retired behind a clump of bushes to attend to a call of nature, and as he was finishing he heard the sound of a motor-cycle coming to a stop. When he emerged into the open he saw a man in leather boots and the uniform of a policeman standing with his hands on his hips and looking at the Volkswagen. The motor-cycle was parked nearby.

Blade walked to the car without undue haste, trying to give an impression of unconcern and doubting whether he was making a very good job of it. The policeman watched him; he was a man of about twenty-five or so wearing a white crash-helmet and his dark, bony features seemed to indicate that there might be a fair sprinkling of Indian blood in his veins. His expression was enigmatic; Blade could read nothing in the eyes, which were deep-set and vigilant.

'Is this your car, señor?' He had a slow, precise way of speaking and his voice had a metallic timbre, as though the words had sharp edges.

'No,' Blade said.

The policeman appeared surprised. 'It is not yours?'

'No. I am a passenger.'

'Then where is the driver?'

'I am here,' Father Rubello said. 'The car is mine.' He had approached unnoticed, beads of water shining on his bald head, a few patches of dampness on his sleeves and chest. 'Have I committed some offence, my son?' His tone was unctuous; it seemed to be implying that if he had erred he was open to correction, possibly prepared even to do some small penance for his sin.

The policeman looked slightly embarrassed; he had obviously not expected to find himself dealing with a priest. His words seemed to lose a little of their sharp-edged quality.

'No offence, Father. I saw the car. It appeared to be abandoned. I felt obliged to investigate.'

Father Rubello smiled benevolently. 'Of course, of course. I see that you are a conscientious man. But the car was not abandoned, merely vacated for a few moments. You understand?'

'I understand, Father.'

Father Rubello continued to smile. The policeman hesitated, still embarrassed but still conscientious. He had his duty to think about.

'I must ask to see your licence, Father.'

'Certainly, my son.' Father Rubello produced the required article without hesitation.

The policeman took a notebook from his pocket and wrote in it. Blade felt uneasy; the man was obviously recording the car's registration number as well as Father Rubello's name. It might be nothing more than routine, but it was disquieting nevertheless. He waited for the policeman to ask him his name, but for the moment the man seemed to have lost interest in him and was more concerned with the car; he strolled round it, peering in through the windows; he asked Father Rubello to open the boot and he looked in there. Blade wondered what he was looking for: weapons, drugs, seditious literature? There was nothing more lethal than a wheel-brace, nothing more seditious than an oily rag.

Father Rubello's smile had faded a little but he showed no uneasiness; his entire bearing proclaimed the fact that he had nothing whatever to hide. The policeman stooped to examine something which had caught his eye at the rear end of the Volkswagen.

'Who has been shooting at you, Father?' he asked.

'Shooting at me!' Father Rubello exclaimed in astonishment. 'What do you mean?'

'Look at this, Father.' The policeman had his finger on a curving part of the bodywork.

Father Rubello went to look and Blade followed, peering over his shoulder. Close to the policeman's fingernail the paint had been chipped away and there was a shallow gouged channel in the metal.

'What would you say that is, Father?'

Father Rubello examined it. 'A scratch in the paintwork. Nothing remarkable. As you can see, the car is old and is not without a few blemishes of one kind and another.'

'But this is new. See how bright the metal is, as if it had been burnished.'

'So perhaps a stone —'

'This doesn't look like the mark a stone would make; it looks more like the result of a bullet glancing off the car.'

It looked like that to Blade, too; the gouge was clean and smooth, with no jaggedness about it. He remembered the whining sound of the ricochet he had heard when Father Rubello fired at the ground to warn the crooked-nosed man that he really meant business. The bullet must have skimmed off a rock or a stone and gone on to make a second ricochet off the metal of the car. Father Rubello might say what he liked, but he was not going to fool the policeman; there was a man who knew a bullet mark when he saw one.

'You don't remember anyone shooting at you?' The policeman looked hard at Father Rubello, and Blade noticed with some misgiving that he no longer seemed embarrassed; perhaps he felt that here was something to justify his questioning.

Father Rubello shook his head. 'No. Who would do such a thing?'

'That is not for me to answer,' the policeman said.

Father Rubello looked at the mark on the car. 'I still think it could have been a stone. A passing truck perhaps — the edge of a heavy tyre passing over the stone — it is squeezed out with the velocity of a bullet leaving the barrel of a gun — such things happen.' He was making it sound as plausible as possible, but Blade felt sure that he too had guessed the real cause of the gouge. It had been a most unfortunate mischance, but such things also happened.

There was disbelief in the policeman's eyes; there was possibly suspicions as well. He could have been reflecting that a car which got itself shot at might be a car to take particular note of. And that could apply to the occupants also. He ran his finger along the gouge as though taking a sensuous pleasure in the act.

'Where have you come from, Father?' he asked.

'From Esperanza.'

'And you did not by chance hear a shot fired during the course of your journey?'

'I can remember none.'

'It is not the kind of thing one would easily forget in so short a time,' the policeman said. He touched the gouge again and gave a faint sigh. 'Well, you may be right; it may have been a stone.'

'It seems most probable,' Father Rubello said.

The policeman did not go so far as to agree with that. He merely said: 'And where are you going, Father?'

Father Rubello's hesitation was so slight as to be almost unnoticeable; but Blade noticed it. He would have said that the policeman noticed it too. He would have said the policeman noticed most things.

'To Nuevo San Tomas. After we have rested and taken some refreshment.'

'You have been there before?'

'On occasion,' Father Rubello said.

'A man would need a good reason to go twice,' the policeman said.

'Perhaps.'

Blade was making himself as inconspicuous as possible and taking no part in the conversation, but he had little hope that this would prevent the policeman from eventually turning the questioning on to him. He was relieved, therefore, and not a little surprised, when the policeman simply walked over to his motor-cycle, started it up and rode away.

Father Rubello shook his head sadly. 'A very suspicious young man, I fear. I don't think he really believed there was any stone. Or any truck either, perhaps.'

'Maybe he would have found it even harder to believe if you had told him it was you who shot at your own car.'

Father Rubello smiled ruefully. 'It was not intentional, I assure you. A chance in a thousand. Who would have thought it?' He touched the gouge with his finger, as the policeman had done. 'And why did we not notice this at once?'

'Possibly because we were not looking for it.'

Father Rubello sighed. 'Yes; and our policeman certainly was looking. Well, there is nothing to be done about it now; we can only go on in the hope that there will be no repercussions. We must put our trust in God.'

'You had better offer up a prayer, Father.'

'I shall do that,' Father Rubello promised. 'Yes, I shall certainly do that.'

Blade would have felt easier in his mind if he had had rather more faith in the efficacy of his companion's prayers, but when you found yourself in a sticky situation any chance of salvation was worth taking. Praying might not do any good, but at least it could do no harm. He might even put in a prayer or two on his own account if he could think of the right words. For had not Father Rubello assured him that God was on their side? It was just too bad that the police appeared to be on the opposite side; not to mention the army and the air force and maybe the navy as well — such as it was.

*

They reached Nuevo San Tomas just as night was falling. Blade had asked Father Rubello why the policeman should have spoken so disparagingly of the town.

'It sounded as if he had a grudge against it.'

Father Rubello had smiled at that. 'Possibly he is stationed there. It is not the kind of place that would be likely to endear itself to a policeman. It is rather rough and raw, and undoubtedly lawless. It has sprung up only recently for the most part; a boom town, you might say. They are building a bridge across the river; it is to be part of a grand new highway. But not everybody wants the bridge or the highway and often there is sabotage. Sometimes the army has to be sent, but the soldiers are not very effective against saboteurs and most of them are needed in the capital to protect the Government and suppress the riots.'

'Why is there opposition to the highway?'

'There are those who say the money could be more usefully spent on other projects which would be of greater benefit to the less privileged people of this country. They say the highway will only put more wealth into the pockets of those who are already rich — the landowners, the big contractors, the bankers, the foreign interests.'

'And what do you think?'

'I think probably they are right. It is not only the North Americans who have their fingers in our affairs now, you know. The Japanese, the Germans and others have moved in. And for whose advantage? Not ours, I fear. They are not here for what they can put in but what they can take out.'

'Why shouldn't it work both ways? If they bring prosperity, surely that should be good for everyone.'

'Admittedly, if it worked like that. Unfortunately, it is good only for the few, the fortunate few who wield the power and skim off the cream for themselves. Anything that remains for the ordinary people is very thin milk indeed.'

Father Rubello had spoken without noticeable vehemence, but Blade had sensed a smouldering fury possessing him. There could be no doubt of the depth of his feeling on this subject.

'But it will not always be so,' he had said. 'Before long there will be great changes in the system. It has happened elsewhere and it will happen here also. The time is coming and it is not far off. Even you, Señor Blade, have a hand in this. You may not admit to any interest in the matter, one way or the other, but you are an instrument nevertheless; an instrument for eventual good.'

\*

From what Blade could see of it in the gathering darkness, Nuevo San Tomas appeared to fit Father Rubello's description. It was certainly rough and raw, a shanty as well as a boom town; the timber buildings set down in no discernible order, overhead cables slung from post to post and making a crazy pattern against the sky. It had begun to rain and there was mud everywhere; light spilled out garishly from the doorways of saloons and eating-houses, and the blaring music of amplifiers could be heard. Already the festivities of the evening appeared to have begun.

'A year ago it was no more than a village,' Father Rubello said. 'Small, of no importance. Now prosperity, of a sort, has hit it; it is a centre of operations. They all come here now — the road-builders, the bridge-builders, the truck-drivers, the camp-followers, the hopefuls seeking a fortune, the gamblers, the parasites; it is a rich stew of humanity; too rich for some stomachs.'

'For yours, Father?'

Rubello smiled. 'A priest must go where he is needed. It is not for him to choose the pleasant paths of life.'

There were cars and lorries, jeeps and covered vans, splashing through the puddles and the mud; there were people moving around on foot, hunched under the falling rain as though the weight of it were bending them down. Father Rubello peered ahead through that segment of the windscreen of the Volkswagen which was swept by the wiper, picking his way with care.

'Where are you taking me?' Blade asked.

'To an establishment where you will be able to get a room.'

'A hotel?'

'Of a sort.'

'And it has to be at this particular place that I get the room?'

'Yes.'

'Why?'

'Because,' Father Rubello said, 'that is the way it has been arranged.'

'And then?'

'I can tell you no more.'

'Or you will not?'

Father Rubello shrugged. 'As you wish.'

It was not as he wished, but he had to accept it; it was no use pressing for information that he was obviously not going to get. And what difference did it make? He had to take events as they came. But when this job was finished things were going to be different; no more of this, ever. This was the final run.

The hotel of a sort presented a dingy, unattractive façade to the street; one naked electric light revealing a sign which stated baldly: 'Rooms'.

Father Rubello stopped the Volkswagen, not directly opposite the entrance, but a short distance beyond it. Blade could hear the rain drumming on the roof of the car and it was a singularly cheerless sound. Across the road a red neon light cast a ruddy glow on the watery scene, imparting a strangely lurid aspect, as though it might have been an anteroom in hell.

'You will ask for room ten,' Father Rubello said.

'Suppose someone has already taken room ten?'

'No one will have taken it.'

'You're sure of that?'

'I am sure.'

'And you?'

'I?'

'What do you do?'

'That is no concern of yours.'

'But you will not be staying here?'

'No.'

'When shall I see you again?'

'That is as God wills. Possibly never. I have done my part in bringing you here.'

Blade saw the pattern: he was being handed on from one guide to another; first Alvarez, then Father Rubello, and who next? He was not sure who this arrangement was designed to baffle, himself or the security forces; it seemed elaborate, perhaps even over-elaborate, but if that was the way they wanted it, that was the way it had to be.

He picked his bag off the rear seat and opened the door of the Volkswagen.

'Goodbye, Father. Perhaps you had better give me your blessing.'

'Willingly, my son.'

The suggestion had been made jestingly, but it was no jest to Father Rubello. He made the sign of the cross with his stubby forefinger.

'Bless you, my son. And God go with you.'

Blade stepped out into the rain wishing he could have believed that Father Rubello's blessing would steer him clear of trouble; you could draw a deal of comfort from belief in a thing like that. The pity of it was that he had no belief.

He slammed the door of the Volkswagen and felt a sense of loss as he watched it move away into the filth of the evening; in the short time he had known them he had developed an odd sort of liking for the car and its owner.

'God go with you too, Father Rubello,' he muttered.

He turned and walked towards the entrance of the hotel of a sort.

# Chapter Eight – Four-Letter Word

There was a counter opposite the door and a bare wooden staircase on the left of it. The lobby itself was as bare as a board; no covering on the floor or the walls, hardly a stick of furniture; the booking-office of a railway station would have promised more comfort.

The clerk behind the counter was past middle age; he had sparse black hair, watery eyes and a nose like a sponge. He looked disillusioned; a man who had lived as long as he had and had attained no better position in life had reason to be disillusioned.

'I want a room,' Blade said.

The clerk looked at him with distaste. 'No rooms,' he said. It seemed to give him a certain vindictive satisfaction to say it, as though he were glad to share some of that disillusionment with a stranger.

'It says rooms on the sign.'

'They're all taken.'

The door opened behind Blade and a girl came in out of the rain. She was wearing a white plastic coat with a hood, and as she came in she pushed the hood back off her head, shedding drops of water on the floor. She had long bleached hair and a lot of make-up, a short, plump body and thick legs. She advanced to the counter on Blade's left and gave the clerk an inquiring look, but without saying anything.

The clerk said briefly: 'Number eleven.'

The girl walked to the stairs and began to climb them, looking back at Blade with an appraising eye. Blade watched her until she had disappeared and then turned again to the clerk.

'I want room ten.'

It seemed to have an effect. The clerk's manner changed miraculously; it was as though some magic word had been spoken; he became suddenly attentive, the watery eyes gazing at Blade with a new interest.

'Room ten, señor? Why that number?'

'It's the one I'm instructed to ask for.'

'Who instructed you, señor?'

'Shall we say a man in black?'

'Ah!' The clerk understood. 'You should have said so at once. Your pardon, señor, but how was I to know?'

'How indeed! And the room is vacant?'

'Of course.'

The clerk took a key from one of a row of hooks behind him and came out through a flapped opening in the counter, shuffling on splayed feet, stooping to pick up Blade's luggage and then going on towards the staircase. He had not bothered about any formality such as the signing of a register.

'Follow me, señor.'

The room was square and Spartan; it was like a box with a bed in it. The clerk placed Blade's bag on the floor.

'It is to your liking, señor?'

'It will do,' Blade said. It would have to do; there was no alternative. And it was unlikely that he would occupy it for long. One night perhaps.

The clerk was hovering. 'If there is anything else, señor — Unfortunately, we do not serve meals, but —'

Blade dismissed him. 'No; nothing else.'

The man went out of the room and shuffled away down the corridor on his splayed feet. He was wearing white canvas shoes which were so worn that his big toes protruded like snails peeping out of their shells.

Blade closed the door and sat down on the bed. He could hear someone moving on the other side of the wooden partition which served as a wall between his room and the next, a low murmur of voices, a sudden burst of gurgling laughter, the creaking of a bed. He guessed that the girl with the bleached hair and the thick legs was in there making some man happy for a while, but it was of no importance; it was no concern of his. There was a small window in the room, curtained with some coarse yellow material. He peered out and could see the red neon sign across the way blazoning in letters three feet high the name — 'Casa Roja'. It looked like a saloon. The rain was still falling. Father Rubello in his white Volkswagen had gone and would not be coming back. He had a feeling of loneliness. He pulled the curtain across the window and sat down on the bed. He heard a door open and shut, the sound of footsteps, someone coughing, the dripping of water. What am I doing here? he thought. How in hell did I get myself into a situation like this?

# Final Run

Father Rubello had given him no hint as to when his next contact would turn up. Possibly he had not known for certain himself when it would be. So it was a question of waiting, waiting.

He put his feet up, lay on the bed and waited. After a while he became aware of hunger and he debated in his mind whether to go out for a meal or leave it until morning. His stomach told him to attend to the matter at once, and since it seemed unlikely that anyone would contact him that evening anyway, he decided to do what the stomach urged.

The clerk was reading a tattered magazine when he went down and dropped his key on the counter. The man looked at him over the top of the magazine.

'You're going out?'

'Yes.'

'Where, señor?'

Blade failed to see why it should be any of the clerk's business where he was going, but he answered civilly: 'I don't know. Does it matter?'

'If someone should ask —'

'Do you think someone will ask?'

'I cannot say. It's possible.'

'Well, if so, tell them I'll be back soon.'

'As you wish, señor.'

It was still raining when he stepped outside and the red neon sign of the Casa Roja was an irresistible attraction. He paused to allow a car to go splashing past, then dashed across the street.

The Casa Roja appeared to be doing good business. There was no lobby; he walked straight into a long room with a long bar and a lot of mirrors reflecting a lot of bottles in serried ranks like soldiers on parade. There was an old juke-box pumping out strident music at the far end of the room, and some of the customers were dancing on a small area of floor with girls who looked as though they went with the place. There were a lot of other customers drinking at tables or propping up the bar, and they seemed a pretty mixed crowd of roughnecks of the kind you usually found doing tough jobs in tough parts of the world. Blade was familiar with the type because he had been one of them; he knew the sort of life they led, the sort of work they did, and the sort of relaxation they demanded at the end of the day. The Casa Roja looked eminently equipped to provide that relaxation.

He walked to the bar and succeeded in attracting the attention of one of the barmen.

'Can I get a meal here?'

The barman indicated with a jerk of the thumb a wide doorway with some faded velvet curtains caught up with cords on either side like the proscenium arch of a stage.

'Dining-room is through there.'

It was almost as big as the other room, but it smelled of food rather than liquor. Blade ordered a grilled steak and it was better than he had expected. He had time to kill and he did not hurry over the meal. When he had finished he went back to the bar and ordered a brandy.

He had finished drinking it when the girl said: 'Are you looking for someone?'

He turned his head to bring her into view and gave her a cool inspection. She was black-haired and dark-skinned, and the rings dangling from the lobes of her ears had the appearance of gold even if they were in fact of some less valuable metal.

'You think I should be?' Blade asked; and it occurred to him that perhaps this was his contact. There had been a leathery-faced man and a priest, so why not now a Casa Roja girl? Nothing would surprise him any more.

'I think you're looking for me,' she said. 'I'm Elena. Maybe you'd like to buy me a drink.'

'Would it be worth my while?'

'There's a way of finding out,' she said. 'Why don't you give it a try?'

He gave it a try. After that he danced with her for a while. She had a good body and the dress she was wearing revealed plenty of it. He could feel her pressing against him as they danced. It had taken him not more than five minutes to come to the conclusion that she was nothing more nor less than what she appeared to be; nevertheless, he found himself toying with the idea of asking her to come back with him to his room and take it from there. But he did no more than toy with it, for he had the sense to realise that it would simply be asking for trouble to get involved with a girl like this. He was in Nuevo San Tomas strictly on business; pleasure had no part in the contract.

He disentangled himself from her arms. 'I've got to go now. It's been nice meeting you.'

She was not pleased about it; he could see that. She had presumably been expecting more from him, a lot more. He would not have been surprised if she had started cursing him and maybe making a scene; but he got away quickly and he was out in the rain before she had time to get going.

# Final Run

The clerk with the nose like a sponge handed him his key. He thought he detected a hint of something in the watery eyes, but the man said nothing so maybe he had imagined it. He went up the stairs and along the corridor to room ten and put the key in the lock, but when he turned it he found that the job had already been done for him. He was not at all sure he liked that; in fact he was dead certain he did not, and he hesitated for a few minutes before making any further move.

But he had to do something and there seemed to be only two alternatives: he could either walk into the room or go down and fetch the sponge-nosed clerk. The latter course of action was not one that he found at all attractive, and perhaps the door was unlocked simply because he had forgotten to lock it when he left the room earlier in the evening. To fetch the clerk because he was afraid to go into his own room might be to expose himself to ridicule, especially if the room proved to be empty. So, all things considered, maybe he had better open the door.

He pushed it open about six inches and he could see that the room was in darkness. He groped for the switch and flicked the light on, and then he pushed the door open fully and saw that he had a visitor.

She was standing with her back to the window and she was wearing a pair of faded jeans and a gabardine jacket with a zip-fastener. He had no idea how long she had been there, but she had certainly been out in the rain, for the jacket was wet and there was a waterproof hat which she had simply dropped on the floor by the bed, and that was wet too.

'Shut the door,' she said, with a trace of urgency in her voice. 'Quickly, please.'

He did so at once, transferring the key from the outside to the inside and turning it in the lock, but keeping a wary eye on the girl as he did so. Then he stood with his back to the door facing her. She had not moved as much as a finger.

'Who are you?' he asked.

'I am Lucia Mandego,' she said, still speaking hurriedly, as though there were no time to waste. 'Where have you been?' It sounded like an accusation.

'If it's any of your business,' Blade said, a little piqued by her tone, 'I've been to get a meal.'

'You should not have gone out. You should have waited here. And it is my business.'

Blade's pique turned to faint amusement at her vehemence. She was of slender build and looked about twenty-five, dark hair trimmed in a kind of urchin style, nose slightly long for her face, mouth wide and eyes full of life and fire.

'I am to take it that you know who I am?'

'I know who you are, Señor Blade; and it was dangerous to go out.'

'Dangerous!'

'Father Rubello has been arrested by the police,' she said. 'It is possible they are already looking for you, since you were seen in the car with him.'

Blade was no longer even faintly amused; it was not an amusing situation. He supposed it must have been the policeman on the motor-cycle who had been responsible; he had probably put in a report concerning the bullet gouge in the Volkswagen and it had built up from there. Perhaps the police had thought of some more questions they wanted to ask Father Rubello; perhaps they were still asking, and maybe getting some answers.

He put a question to the girl: 'How do you know he has been arrested?'

She answered impatiently: 'I had just left him; just left the house. I saw the police arrive. I saw them take him away. They took the car also.'

'You must have had a narrow escape yourself.'

'Yes, but that is not important. Now we must go. Are you ready?'

He had not even unpacked his bag; there was nothing to delay his departure. But still he hesitated. Could he trust this girl? What proof did he have that she was not perhaps an agent of the police herself? He dismissed the idea as absurd; it simply did not fit into the pattern; she had to be his contact.

She picked up the waterproof hat and put it on. 'Shall we go? Or do you wish to wait for the police?'

He had no wish to do that. He wondered how much Father Rubello knew. Perhaps he would refuse to talk; but most people did talk eventually — under pressure.

He stooped and picked up the bag that was all his luggage. 'All right; let's be on our way.'

There was no one in the corridor. Lucia Mandego went first; Blade closed the door and followed. They came to the head of the stairs and stopped abruptly. Blade could hear a man's voice coming up from the lobby, a voice he did not recognise. Then the clerk was answering, and he seemed to be protesting about something.

The girl bent down and peered through the banisters, then straightened quickly and stepped back, treading on Blade's toes. She turned and spoke to him in an urgent whisper.

'Go back. It's the police.'

They retreated from the stairs as soundlessly as possible and were back at the room.

'How many were there?' Blade asked.

'Two.'

'They didn't see you?'

'They didn't look up. One of them was questioning the clerk; the other was examining the register.'

'My name isn't in it.'

'That's not going to help. They're bound to search the place.'

'So what do you suggest we do?'

'We must get out some other way. Come on.'

She was tugging at his sleeve and he allowed himself to be led by her, since she seemed to know what she was doing. It was not a long corridor and they soon reached the far end. At this point there was a branch to the right terminating in another staircase, narrow and twisting and practically in darkness. With the girl still in the lead they began to descend just as an outbreak of shouting and banging on doors came from the corridor behind them. It was obvious that the police were starting to search the rooms and the shrill sounds of protesting female voices indicated that the operation was not proving altogether unproductive.

Lucia was feeling her way down the staircase and Blade, with his bag in his hand, was pressing closely behind her. At the bottom they came to a halt. There was an unpleasant sickly odour of damp and decaying wood and bad drains, while a dim rectangle on one side gave a faint suggestion of light and was evidently a window in the rear of the building.

'There must be a door,' Blade whispered. 'I'll try to find it.'

He moved towards the window and his foot struck something which rolled away with a metallic clatter — a bucket or tin of some sort. The noise seemed as loud as a brass band suddenly striking up and set his pulse going like a steam-hammer.

'Take care,' the girl said, and he could feel her hand gripping his arm.

They were both absolutely still for a moment, listening intently. The sounds of thumping and shouting came distantly from the floor above, but there was no indication that the clatter of the tin had been heard through the racket that was going on overhead.

Blade moved forward again towards the window and was stopped abruptly by something hard and unyielding which caught him rather painfully just below the stomach. Groping with his free hand he discovered a cool damp surface and realised that it must be a sink. He shifted to the right and still groping with his outstretched hand discovered the unmistakable outline of a door.

'It's here,' he said. 'I've found it.' And then: 'But it's locked.'

He could feel the girl close beside him and he knew that she was also tracing the contours of the door with her hand.

Suddenly she said: 'It's bolted.'

He could hear her wrestling with a bolt somewhere near the level of his head. He bent down and found another bolt at the foot of the door; it made a screeching sound as he drew it back. The girl was having difficulty with the upper bolt. There was very little noise coming from the floor above now, and that seemed ominous.

'Let me do it,' he said.

He set the bag down and seized the bolt in both hands. It was stiff and probably rusty, but he exerted all the pressure he could and it shot back suddenly with a loud click. He found the doorknob, turned it and pulled; the door resisted for a moment before coming open with a kind of shudder and a scud of rain drove in. At almost the same instant a light appeared at the head of the stairway and a man's voice said:

'What's down there?'

Blade failed to catch the reply; it was muffled and he was busy pushing the girl through the doorway, picking up his bag and following her. He closed the door behind them as gently as he could just as the heavy tread of feet could be heard on the stairs.

'Better get away from here quick,' he said. 'They're coming.'

They were in a narrow alleyway, muddy underfoot and illuminated only by the glimmer of light that was coming from a curtained window here and there. Lucia had taken the lead again and they started off at a run, splashing through the mud and with the rain falling now in a steady downpour.

They had gone about twenty paces when the door by which they had left the building was pulled open, and Blade, glancing back over his shoulder, saw one of the policemen silhouetted in the doorway by the light which had been switched on behind him. The man must at the same moment have caught a glimpse of them running away and he shouted something which, though indistinct, could only have been an order to halt. Far from obeying the order, however, they merely increased their pace; and then the second policeman appeared and both of them set off in pursuit.

Blade was hampered by the bag he was carrying, but the end of the alleyway was not far ahead and he was hopeful that they would reach it before the policemen caught up with them. But what then? The alleyway could only open into a road or street, and it was unlikely that they could evade their pursuers for long. Moreover, the very fact of having run away would make it useless to protest innocence if they were caught; what stronger evidence of guilt could there be than flight from the police?

And then he became aware of something else; something which made the question of what lay beyond the end of the alleyway entirely academic, since it was highly unlikely that they would ever get as far as that. A jeep with the hood up had just moved into position across the alleyway, completely blocking the exit. He had scarcely had time to take in the implication of this new factor when another thing happened: one of the pursuing policemen opened up with a pistol.

It seemed an unnecessary thing to do, since it was now all too obvious that they were trapped anyway, but perhaps the man got a kick out of using his gun and would be just as happy to take a dead prisoner as a live one. He was shooting with an unpleasant degree of accuracy, too; a bullet slapped into the mud no more than an inch or two from Blade's right foot. The sensation as of cold water trickling down the spine was not caused by the rain but by something altogether different, something that could have been described in one little four-letter word — fear. It was not the first time he had been shot at, not by a long chalk; but familiarity with the process had never made a pennyworth of difference to the effect it had on him; it still gave him a sick feeling in the pit of the stomach that set that cold-water tap dribbling down his spine.

So what in hell did they do now? With the way ahead sealed off and a maniac with a gun coming up fast behind. Or maybe two maniacs with two guns, since the other policeman might at any moment take it into his thick head to get in on the shooting act as well. It certainly looked like the final run all right, the final run with a vengeance.

And then he felt the girl give a tug on his right arm and heard her sing out sharply: 'This way! Quick!'

There was a wooden fence on the left and he saw her slip through a gap like a rabbit going down a hole. A bullet smacked into the timber and he waited for nothing more; he shoved his bag through the gap and went in after it. The girl had gone through easily but it was a tight squeeze for him because he was bigger, and he thought for one horrible moment that he was going to be stuck, unable to move forward or back, a sitting duck for anyone who cared to take a shot at him. The cold water in his spine was rapidly turning to ice, but he gave a desperate heave and went through like a pip being squeezed out of an orange and tripped over his bag and went down on to his hands and knees in more mud. Bloody hell, he thought, who would be a commercial traveller when there were nice safe cosy public lavatories in need of attendants?

Lucia was tugging impatiently at his shoulder, helping him to get to his feet; though in fact he needed no help to do that, and no urging either; not with those bastards on the other side of the fence.

'Come on! Hurry!'

He got up and grabbed his bag, and he could see that they were in what appeared to be the yard of a saw-mill. There was a fair amount of light coming from a large low building not far away which revealed some shadowy open sheds, stacks of sawn boards and piles of rough logs.

The girl began to run again and he followed, the mud almost ankle-deep in places and clinging glutinously to his shoes. He heard a shout behind him, and when he turned his head he could see the leading policeman trying to force his way through the gap in the fence; but he was a big man and he was finding it an even more difficult operation than Blade had. He had got his head and one arm through, and the hand on the end of the arm was the one that was holding the gun. He fired a couple of shots but they were well off target, and after that he seemed to run out of ammunition.

Lucia stopped suddenly and turned, thrust a hand inside her gabardine jacket and hauled out a small pistol of her own. She held the pistol in both hands and loosed off three shots in the direction of the fence in rapid succession. Blade was not sure whether the policeman was hit or whether he was merely scared by the bullets slapping into the timber too close for comfort, but he gave a yell and disappeared very promptly from the gap. Blade was impressed by the girl's shooting, but he had no time to compliment her on it because she had stowed the gun away and was on the move again. He fell in behind and got the benefit of the mud being kicked up by her heels.

They took a turning to the left and ran on between two tall stacks of timber, and then turned right again and about thirty yards further on came to another fence. It was some ten or a dozen feet high and there were no gaps as far as Blade could see. But it was difficult to see anything, since there was very little light penetrating to this part of the yard. He could hear a lot of shouting and he guessed that the policemen had managed to break in, but they seemed to be some distance away and were possibly searching among the sheds and timber stacks.

'We shall have to climb it,' Lucia said. 'Help me up.'

Blade put down his bag, took a hold on the girl's legs and lifted her until she could get her hands on the top of the fence. She was no great load, and in a moment she had hauled herself up and was sitting astride the barrier.

'Give me your bag,' she said; and she sounded very cool, he thought, for someone who had a couple of policemen on her tail and had just taken a few pot-shots at one of them.

He handed up the bag and she said: 'Can you manage now?'

'I can manage,' he said.

The vertical boards of the fence were nailed to horizontal rails, and he got his foot on the bottom rail and gave a heave and he could just reach to the top with his fingers. A moment later he was on the other side with the girl.

'Are you feeling all right?' she asked; and he noticed that she sounded quite concerned about him. Which was nice.

In fact he was feeling pretty lousy to say the least, and the rain was not helping much. He was muddy and scared and a trifle sick in the guts, and what he would have liked most of all at that moment was a good hot bath followed by about eight hours of undisturbed sleep in a comfortable bed. But he doubted whether there was even the remotest chance of getting anything of the kind, so he would probably just have to go on feeling lousy for quite a while yet.

'Oh, I'm fine,' he said. 'This is just the kind of thing I enjoy most of all. An evening out with a charming companion. Who could ask for more?'

She ignored the sarcasm. 'It's not far now. Come along; we'll soon be there.'

He wondered where 'there' was, and he doubted whether he would find it altogether pleasing when he got the answer; but she had set off again at a cracking pace and he had no choice but to follow her.

## Chapter Nine – Idyllic

It turned out to be even worse than he had imagined. He would never have had a hope of finding it by himself, not in a thousand years, even if he had known what he was looking for; but he had just stuck close to the girl and she had led him through an intricate pattern of unpaved alleyways and footpaths until they had come to the river. They seemed to have successfully shaken off the police and they had got to the river with no further cause for alarm.

It was a large canoe or boat and it was about half a kilometre upstream, drawn up against the bank and practically invisible. He would not have noticed himself, but Lucia, in addition to her other attributes, seemed to have the eyesight of a cat, and she spotted it quickly enough.

'This is it,' she said.

Having had it pointed out to him, Blade could just discern the dark shape of the canoe. He thought it was empty until something stirred with a rustle of waterproof sheeting and a few words were muttered in a man's voice, very low and cautious. Blade failed to catch what was said, but Lucia apparently understood, for she answered immediately:

'All right, Pedro. We are here.'

'Ah,' the man said; and the sheet rustled again as he moved in the canoe. He spoke with less caution and in a faintly grumbling tone. 'It is time. You had trouble?'

'A little. But we are here now and ready to go.' She turned to Blade. 'Get into the canoe.'

Blade hesitated and she said sharply: 'There is no time to waste.'

Again he detected that note of urgency in her voice, and guessed that she was more nervous than she would have had him believe. He was rather glad of that; it made two of them who were nervous. He was not sure whether Pedro also was nervous, but it seemed likely; there was quite a lot to be nervous about.

He handed his bag down into the canoe and lowered himself carefully after it. The canoe felt alarmingly unstable and he crouched down in the bottom while Lucia got in. Pedro cast off from the bank and gave a push with his hand, and the canoe moved out into the river.

Blade had not been aware that there was an outboard motor on the stern until Pedro started it. It came to life with a frenzied popping sound and the canoe surged forward. Pedro pointed the bows up-river and the lights of Nuevo San Tomas gradually receded behind them.

Blade hoped Pedro could see where he was going; it seemed to him that they were heading into impenetrable murk. He thought uneasily of such things as mud-banks and floating logs and even alligators; especially of alligators. The rain continued to pour down and nobody seemed to be in the mood for idle chatter; it was hardly that kind of party. He had asked Lucia where they were going and had received as much information on that point as he ever seemed to get.

'You'll see.'

'Not in this lot. I can't see a damned thing.'

'There's another day tomorrow,' she said.

He just hoped he would be alive to see it.

It seemed to go on for a long time. After an hour or so he stopped looking at his watch and simply crouched there in utter misery, mentally cursing himself for ever letting Korvan talk him into this business. Even for ten thousand pounds it was not worth it; and maybe he would never get the money anyway; there were so many things that could go wrong, and some of them already had.

He caught himself thinking about the girl, Lucia Mandego. What was she in it for? Well, he was pretty sure he knew the answer to that one; she was serving a cause — like Alvarez and Father Rubello, like the man he had come to bargain with and had not yet seen. These people who were wedded to a cause scared him; they put too low a value on their lives — and on the lives of others; they would take any kind of risk to achieve their aims. He himself disliked risks; and he valued his life and gave not a damn about any cause under the sun; all he wanted was to make his little pile and get out with a whole skin. And the sooner the better.

It was almost as though the girl had been reading his thoughts. She asked suddenly:

'Have you always been in this kind of business, Señor Blade?'

'Not always,' Blade said.

'And why are you in it now?'

'For the money.'

'And nothing else?'

'What else should I be in it for?'

'You never trouble yourself with concern for the poor and the downtrodden, the deprived and the persecuted, the starving and the destitute?'

'I don't take it upon myself to change the world, if that's what you mean. And besides —'

'Besides, Señor Blade?'

'What happens when the poor and the downtrodden turn the tables? When they get on top. Very soon they become oppressors themselves. It's happened often enough — in France, Russia, China, all over the world. It's human nature and you can't change that. Revolutions solve nothing.'

'Do you really have such a poor opinion of your fellow men?'

'Not all of them, no; there are some good men.'

'But the majority are bad? Is that your opinion?'

'Judging by the present state of the world it might not be far off the mark.'

She was silent for a while, as though turning his words over in her mind. Then she said: 'You are wrong, of course. You take too cynical a view. Yet somehow I don't think you are really as cynical as you try to make me believe.'

'I'm not trying to make you believe anything.'

'Well, perhaps not,' she said; and after that she lapsed again into silence.

Blade had fallen into a kind of sodden revery when he was roused by the stopping of the motor. He looked around him and could still see nothing much through the murky blanket of darkness. The rain was falling as steadily as ever and he could hear it pattering on the surface of the water. But then the canoe nosed gently into a soft bank and he felt his cheek brushed by what could have been wet leaves. Lucia was doing something at the prow of the boat and he came to the conclusion that she must be making the canoe fast to the bank. A moment or two later she finished what she was doing and moved back to the centre of the canoe.

'Don't tell me we're home already,' Blade said.

She ignored the sourness in his tone. 'We shall go no further tonight. It is too difficult in the dark — and dangerous. We shall start again as soon as it gets light.'

'You mean we're to stay here — in the boat?'

'You can get out if that is what you wish, but I don't advise it. I think you will be more comfortable where you are.'

'You call this comfort?'

'It could be worse, you know.'

He supposed she must mean that they might have been caught by the police; he could see no other way in which things could have been worse: the rain gave no indication of slackening and there was water in the bottom of the canoe. It looked like being a long and miserable night.

There was a rustling sound behind him; it was Pedro manipulating the waterproof sheet. Lucia told him to stay where he was while she and Pedro fixed up an awning over the canoe. It was an awkward job in the darkness and Blade felt himself to be very much in the way. It seemed there were some light wooden crutches to be erected, and then the waterproof sheet was draped over them to form a kind of low, narrow tent. It could not have been described as luxurious accommodation, but at least it was better than being exposed to the weather. The rain made a constant drumming sound on the cover, the monotony of which was varied only by slight changes in the intensity of the tattoo.

There was no room to stand up even if anyone had wished to do so. Blade sat with his knees drawn up almost to his chin and his shoulders resting against the side of the canoe; he had to keep his head bowed, because if he lifted it he came into contact with the awning. He felt wet and cramped and wretched, and he had no hope whatever of getting a wink of sleep. Nevertheless, he must have dozed off, for he woke suddenly to find someone moving beside him. For a moment he had only a hazy awareness of where he was, but it came back to him very quickly and gave him no great pleasure when it did. He was conscious of an aching neck and a general stiffness in the limbs as a result of his cramped position.

'What is it?' he said, making no attempt to keep the snappishness out of his voice. 'What's wrong now?'

It was the girl who answered. 'Oh, I'm sorry. Were you asleep? I shouldn't have awakened you.'

She was very close to him; when she moved again he felt her leg touch his.

'Maybe you did the right thing at that,' he said in a more friendly tone. 'My neck could have become permanently locked.' He massaged it with his hand, trying to work the crick out of it. 'Has anything happened?'

'No; nothing.'

'What time is it?'

'Nearly three.'

'As late as that! It'll soon be morning.'

'Yes. Very soon now.'

He noticed something which had not impressed itself on his consciousness until that moment: there was no longer any continuous drumming sound on the awning; only now and then a brief patter as of drops falling from overhanging foliage.

'The rain has stopped.'

'About half an hour ago.'

'I must have slept longer than I realised. But you stayed awake?'

'There'll be time for sleep later.'

The sound of her voice coming out of the darkness was strangely exciting; he felt his pulse quicken a little at the sense of her nearness, an invisible presence at his side; even the pressure of the damp gabardine as her shoulder touched his set up a tingling in the blood. Which was all very foolish and something a man of his experience should have been proof against; yet apparently was not.

He shifted his position, trying to ease the cramp in his limbs, and again there was that contact, again the tingle of excitement. He wondered whether she was conscious of it too.

He wanted her to go on talking, wanted to hear her voice, low-pitched, warm, very close to him, as if her lips were almost touching his ear even though he could not see her face. His fear was that she would move away from him again; he wanted her to stay where she was and go on talking, talking.

'What are you thinking about?' she asked.

He answered truthfully: 'About you.'

She laughed softly. 'That is hardly an interesting subject.'

'On the contrary; it is very interesting.'

'In what way?'

'In all kinds of ways. Let's talk about it.'

He heard the sound of movement in the stern of the canoe. Pedro was awake, but he was saying nothing; he seemed to be a taciturn man. But perhaps he was listening.

'What do you wish to know about me, Señor Blade?'

'Everything. And my name is Frank.'

'To tell everything might take time, Francisco,' she said; and laughed again, very softly.

'We have time, Lucia. And what else is there to do?'

Later he stretched out his arm and pulled her to him. He found her lips in the darkness and she did not draw away. He could hear Pedro coughing faintly as though to remind them that he was still there.

*

For breakfast they had canned Coca-Cola and biscuits from a tin. Blade detested Coca-Cola but he was thirsty and the river water looked unfit to drink. The canoe was in a narrow inlet in the bank of an island; it was overhung by rampant vegetation, completely hidden from view. At the first glimmer of daylight they had removed the awning and had taken the hasty meal. Pedro topped up the fuel tank from a can of petrol and a few minutes later the motor was popping and they were on their way.

Tangled jungle growth on each side of the river formed high green walls which restricted the view to no more than that stretch of water which lay between one bend and the next. The sun rose quickly, sucking up clouds of steam, and a constant chattering sound of birds and animals came from the impenetrable shadows of the trees. Here and there alligators floated half-submerged or lay stretched out on the mud like scaly submarines waiting to be launched.

Pedro steered the canoe, sitting in the stern as expressionless as a carven idol. He was a short, thick-set man with sloping shoulders and long arms. His skin was of a dark coppery hue and he had a nose like the beak of a bird of prey. He looked as if he had more Indian blood in him than any other variety, and he was certainly taciturn; he spoke only when spoken to, and used his words sparingly even then.

Blade found himself continually glancing at Lucia Mandego, but he could detect no indication in her manner that her thoughts were on what had passed between them a few hours previously. There was no hint of any particular meaning in her glance, but he thought she looked happy, as though she had not a care in the world.

'You're very cheerful this morning,' he said.

She smiled at him. 'And why not, Francisco? It is a very pleasant morning.'

He noticed that she still addressed him by the Spanish version of his name. It was a whim, but he rather liked it. And it proved that she had not completely forgotten their conversation in the small hours.

'I hope it brings no unpleasantness later,' he said.

'I am sure it will not. Everything will be fine now. You will see.'

'I hope so; but I wouldn't bet on it.'

'You are too pessimistic. You should look at the bright side of things.'

'Such as?'

'That the sun is shining; that your clothes are drying; that you are going to make a lot of money. You are, are you not?'

'Maybe. But I'll tell you what is the brightest side of things right now.'

She looked at him with a questioning expression. 'Yes?'

'You are.'

She gave a delighted laugh. 'Then you must look at me, Francisco. Isn't that so?'

'It will be no hardship,' Blade said. 'No hardship at all, believe me.'

A little later they came to the confluence of the main river and a smaller one. Pedro steered the canoe into the minor stream and they went on with the banks nearer at hand and the jungle shutting them in ever more closely. It was apparent now why it would have been impracticable to have travelled further in the night: if they had not missed the fork in the river altogether, the way would have been made increasingly hazardous by mud-banks and shoals, fallen trees and snags of various kinds. Pedro steered with skill between these many obstacles, while the river twisted like a snake, the engine chattered like a garrulous old man and the hours of the morning wore slowly away.

They came to the village in the afternoon. It was not a large settlement; no more than a scattering of thatched huts in a clearing, with some patches of cultivated ground adjoining it. There were some canoes drawn up out of the water and as soon as they arrived a small concourse of villagers — men, women and children — crowded down to the river bank to greet them.

'Is this where I meet my man?' Blade asked.

'This is where you meet him,' Lucia said. 'But not today.'

'No? Then when?'

'When he comes.'

'And how long will that be?'

'Who knows? Does it worry you?'

'I'd like to get it finished.'

'But why be in such a hurry?' she said. 'You will find it pleasant enough here, I am sure. It's really quite idyllic, don't you think?'

'An idyll is not exactly what I came for. Will you also be staying here?'

'For the present, yes.'

Blade surveyed the scene — the placid river glinting in the sunlight, the tangled jungle vegetation, the picturesque thatched huts, the apparently friendly people — and he had to admit that idyllic was an apt description. His gaze returned to Lucia Mandego, who would be staying there also for the present.

'Well,' he said, 'it may not be so bad at that. It may not be so bad at all.'

## Chapter Ten – Shopping List

They had obviously been expected. Blade found that a hut had been allotted to him; it was furnished with a hammock and very little else. It was Spartan accommodation, but what more could one expect? And it would be only for a few days, unless there should be some unforeseen delay.

He wondered how the information that he was at the rendezvous would be conveyed to the person it concerned. Perhaps a messenger — one of the villagers maybe — would go on foot bearing the message. And how far would the man have to travel? He supposed he might ask Lucia about that, but she would probably not tell him if he did. It was not important; what difference did a few days more or less make? But he would be glad to have the whole thing finished; glad to be out of it.

He could not remember when he had last slept in a hammock; it must have been years ago; and when he climbed into the thing and heard the posts between which it was slung start to creak he wondered whether it was going to be hard to doze off. But there had been no need to worry on that score; the last time he had had a night's sleep in a bed had been at the Hotel Segovia in Quintuaquintzl, and even that had not been altogether satisfactory. He had slept a little in Alvarez's car and in a chair at the house in Esperanza, and he had snatched a few brief catnaps in the canoe, but the lot added up to a something a long way short of his normal ration. The result was that he had scarcely hoisted himself into the hammock and closed his eyes before he was well away.

It was Lucia who woke him. It was broad daylight and she had given the hammock a push, so that it was swinging a little and making the posts creak.

'Are you planning to sleep all day?' she asked. 'Half the morning's gone.'

He looked at his watch. She had exaggerated slightly, but he had certainly made up for that lost sleep.

'Has anything moved?'

'No,' she said; 'nothing's moved. You must try not to be so impatient.' She gave him a critical inspection, her head tilted a little to one side, smiling slightly, as though she found some cause for amusement in what she saw.

Blade was a trifle nettled. 'Well, what's so funny? Have you never seen a man in a hammock before?'

'It has nothing to do with the hammock,' she said. 'I was just thinking that you are not looking quite at your best. If you don't mind me saying so, you could use a comb and a razor.'

Blade fingered the stubble on his chin and did a bit of inspecting on his own account. If he did not look his best, the same could certainly not be said of her; unless her best was really something quite remarkable. He decided that his first impression had not done her justice; she was really quite a girl.

'Maybe I should grow a beard. It would be less trouble.'

She shook her head emphatically. 'No; a beard would not suit you. You are not the type.'

'You think not?'

'I am sure not. So now you had better get up and shave. Would you like me to fetch you some water?'

'Do I have any breakfast?'

'Breakfast, yes. But first the shave.'

'Are you giving me orders?'

'Yes; I am giving you orders.'

'You'd make a hell of a wife,' Blade said. 'You'd have a man right under your thumb.'

She gave a laugh and went away to fetch the water.

*

He felt better after the shave. He felt better still after the breakfast, even if it was no cordon bleu meal. A man with an appetite such as his was not fussy regarding what he ate as long as it was wholesome and satisfying.

'And how,' he asked, 'does one pass the time in a place like this?'

Her eyes seemed to mock him. 'There speaks the urban man, the product of so-called civilisation. You think there can be nothing but boredom away from the cinemas and the theatres, the saloons and the television, all the other clutter of city life.'

'Maybe you're wrong,' Blade said. 'Maybe I'm not so urban at that. I was raised on a farm.'

'An English farm? All fully mechanised and within twenty kilometres of the nearest town? That would be a long way from this kind of thing.'

'It would be,' Blade admitted. 'But let me ask you this — were you brought up in these conditions? You don't strike me as being much of a peasant yourself.'

It seemed to take her a little out of her stride and she was not immediately ready with a reply. Blade pressed his advantage.

'Tell me, where were you born?'

She answered with a certain reluctance, as though confessing to some secret vice: 'In Mexico City.'

'And what could be more urban than that? But Mexico is another country. How did you get yourself mixed up in this lot?'

'My parents moved out of Mexico — for certain reasons.'

'Political reasons?'

'Yes.'

'And now they're living here? Do they know what you're doing? Do they approve?'

'If they were alive,' she said, 'I am sure they would approve.'

'They're dead? I'm sorry.'

'They were executed for activities inimical to the State. That was the wording of the charge.'

'Oh, I see. They were revolutionaries too.'

'Not of a violent kind; they were very gentle people. My father was a professor of sociology and believed in freedom of speech. In this country that kind of belief can cost a man his life — and a woman hers also.' She smiled a trifle grimly. 'In that respect at least we have equality of the sexes.'

Blade regretted having steered the conversation into these regions; it seemed to have cast a shadow over the morning, and he wanted no shadows. It had not been his intention to bring back the memory of past tragedy to the girl's mind; but he could understand better now why she should be so strongly attached to the revolutionary cause; she had good reason not to love a Government that had executed her parents.

He changed the subject.

'Why was this place chosen for the rendezvous?'

'Why not? It is as good as any other.'

'And the villagers are to be trusted?'

'It is in their interests that we should succeed in our struggle. Why should they betray us?'

Blade was not sure he would have considered it a sufficient guarantee of good faith; people could show a surprising lack of gratitude to those who fought for their welfare. But perhaps the villagers were trustworthy. He hoped so — for Lucia's sake as well as his own.

He spent the rest of the morning in her company. They seemed to be accepted by the community without question; even the natural curiosity regarding two persons so obviously different from the native inhabitants quickly wore off, or perhaps was concealed from motives of innate courtesy. Pedro had disappeared and there was no sign of the canoe with the outboard motor. It occurred to him that perhaps Pedro had gone to fetch the man with whom he was to do business, but when he suggested this to Lucia she remained reticent.

'Never mind where Pedro has gone. I told you you must be patient.'

'I am being patient,' Blade said. 'I just hope the man comes.'

'He will come. You don't suppose we've brought you here simply for amusement, do you?'

'It would be strange amusement.'

'Yes, very strange. But never fear; he will come.'

'I believe you. After all, you need me as much as I need you. It cuts both ways.'

*

In the afternoon he dozed in the hammock. When he woke he left the hut and went to look for Lucia, feeling a sense of loss without her company. She was nowhere to be seen around the village and he discovered her eventually bathing naked in a shallow pool some distance upstream.

He was enchanted by the sight; she was like a naiad with her dripping hair, her perfect breasts, her smooth skin glistening with silver drops of water, and the laughter in her eyes. She seemed entirely unembarrassed by his presence; not flaunting her body but rather as though utterly unaware of it.

'Why don't you join me?'

'Is this part of the idyll?' he asked.

She made a sweeping gesture with her arm, scattering the silver drops. 'Wouldn't you say it was idyllic?'

'Nothing could be more so. And no alligators?'

'No alligators. What are you waiting for?'

It was an invitation he found irresistible. He stripped quickly and waded into the pool. The girl watched him.

'You are very well made,' she said with disarming candour.

'I'm glad you think so.'

'I was stating a fact, not giving an opinion.'

'And I could say the same about you.'

'I know,' she said, a hint of amusement in her voice. 'We are very well matched, you and I, don't you think?'

'Very well matched indeed.'

'And that is fortunate. It makes things so much more pleasant, doesn't it? I mean, if we're going to spend a few days together it wouldn't be nearly as enjoyable if one of us — or even both — were physically repulsive, would it?'

'No,' Blade said; 'it wouldn't.'

'Now do you think we ought to swim a little?'

'If you wish.'

They swam a little. They splashed each other in the warm shallows, playing like children. Blade forgot for a while the real purpose for which he was there and surrendered to the idyll. This girl, so divinely enchanting, filled his thoughts to the exclusion of all else, while she for her part seemed to be revelling joyfully in this brief silvan interlude.

They let the sun dry them.

'I am not sure,' Blade said, 'that I want the man to come. Not yet.'

She looked at him with the laughter in her eyes. 'No?'

'No.'

'But he will come,' she said. 'He will not delay it for your pleasure. Or mine.'

He could not imagine why he had ever thought her nose too long; it seemed perfect now. Everything about her was perfect; there was no way she could have been improved; not in his eyes.

'Now what is in your mind?' she asked.

'You know what is in my mind,' he said. 'And I think perhaps it is in your mind too.'

'Perhaps it is.' Of a sudden her breathing seemed to quicken, to catch in her throat. 'And there is so little time. There is always so little time.'

'We can use what time there is,' he said.

'Yes,' she said; 'we can do that.'

\*

Later they swam again. He was captivated by this girl, this naiad, and could not wrench his gaze away from her. Again he wondered when the man would come, and hoped it would not be soon. One more day, two days, three? It could not be too long, could not be long enough; a century would not be long enough.

'I love you,' he said. 'That's the way it is. I love you. There's no damned use denying it.'

'You think so,' she said, 'for the moment. But the moment will pass. You will soon forget. When you have gone from here I shall slip out of your mind like a dream. It will not last. That's the way things are. You must know it is.'

He thought he detected a note of regret, as though she wished it might be different but was too honest with herself to believe that it could be.

'No,' he said; 'you are wrong. I shall not forget. I love you.'

'You have known me for less than two days. How can you say you love me?'

'It's not a question of time. Time doesn't count.'

She looked at him, unsmiling now. 'You are really serious, aren't you?'

'I am serious,' Blade said.

She gave a sigh. 'But it makes no difference. It can't last. You know that.'

He did not argue with her. He was not so blinded that he could fail to see all the snags, all the reasons why there could be no future in it. And maybe she had been right in saying that he would forget after a while. And yet he loved her; that was the truth; he did love her. That was the hell of it.

'I hope the man never comes,' he said.

She sighed again. 'He will come. Soon.'

\*

He came on the third day. Pedro brought him. He was a big heavy man of forty with a growing paunch. He was dressed in an olive-green shirt and a long-peaked cap, trousers tucked into jungle boots. He had a Castro beard and curly black hair and hard, suspicious eyes. He shook hands with Blade, and the hand was rough and calloused, perhaps from handling guns. He introduced himself.

'I am Raimundo Lecaros.'

Blade nodded. 'I am Frank Blade.'

He studied Lecaros with interest, this man who hoped to overthrow the established Government as Castro had done in Cuba. Lecaros looked capable of doing so; he had the confident manner of a leader; he had perhaps what is popularly known as charisma. But that was no guarantee of success; it took more than that; it took modern weapons and men trained to use them. Well, it was weapons that this meeting was all about, and no doubt Lecaros could provide the men.

There was another man with him, lithe, dark-skinned, narrow-faced, intense-looking, his eyes restless, missing nothing. He was also introduced to Blade; his name was Diego Saurez. He shook hands perfunctorily, with a kind of disdain, as though in his heart he despised such a bourgeois act; perhaps even despised Blade also.

They went to the hut that had been allotted to Blade. Lecaros seemed to be in a hurry to get down to business; perhaps he did not feel altogether safe there and wanted to get away as quickly as possible. Lucia came with them. There were no chairs; they squatted on their haunches, using the floor for a table.

It was Saurez who had what Lecaros referred to as the shopping list. They knew precisely what they wanted — sub-machine-guns, automatic rifles, anti-tank weapons, grenades, ammunition. Blade had his own list; it was a price list in code; it looked like a letter from a friend; if it had fallen into the wrong hands it would have betrayed nothing. He translated it into weapons and dollars. Lecaros and Saurez looked at each other, frowned and shook their heads. The prices were too high.

'They are as low as it is possible to make them,' Blade said. 'There is the cost of delivery to be taken into account. And the risk.'

'There is no risk,' Lecaros said.

'That is a matter of opinion. But there has to be a reasonable profit; Señor Korvan is not interested in charity; he is a man of business.'

'We do not ask for charity,' Saurez said, with a touch of anger; and it seemed to Blade that for two pins this vitriolic man would have jumped up and been at his throat.

Lecaros put a hand on his lieutenant's arm as though to restrain him from violence. 'We ask only for fair dealing,' he said. 'These prices are too high. Come, you must realise that yourself, Señor Blade. You are not a fool.'

Blade saw that the bargaining had begun. It was not to be expected that they would agree to the asking price without a quibble, and he was not surprised that they had jibbed. He prepared himself for a bout of haggling.

'And what,' he asked cautiously, 'would you suggest as fair?'

Lecaros and Saurez went into brief consultation and came up with some figures which Blade had no doubt at all they would have been amazed if he had accepted; it was all part of the game.

'Señores,' he said, with a smile of disbelief, 'you have surely not brought me all this way merely to talk nonsense. If so, I may as well go home at once.' He got to his feet, not simply as a gesture of disgust with their offer but also because his legs were beginning to protest at the squatting position. He even walked as far as the doorway of the hut before Lecaros called him back.

'Do not go, Señor Blade; I am sure we can come to an amicable arrangement.'

Blade returned to his place and the bargaining continued. It eventually concluded with Lecaros and Saurez accepting with a certain show of reluctance prices that were twenty per cent lower than those which Blade had originally demanded. For his part he was well satisfied. Korvan had authorised him to knock off a maximum of thirty per cent if necessary and he had done a lot better than that. He made a note of the quantities required and added up the total cost. It came to one million, one thousand and eight hundred dollars. Saurez checked the figures and then they got down to the question of delivery.

Saurez produced a map and spread it out on the ground between them. He took a pencil from his pocket and marked a point on the coastline.

'There.'

Blade examined the map. Where Saurez had made the mark there appeared to be a small inlet from the sea, perhaps a natural harbour.

'It is safe there?' he asked; and he was not referring to navigational hazards.

Lecaros understood what he meant. 'We shall make it safe. As you can see, there is a small fishing village. My men will occupy the village and cut off all communications.'

'You can do that?'

'For as long as it takes to discharge the cargo. The people will not resist; why should they? We are their friends.'

'I hope they know that.'

'They know it. Correct timing will, of course, be essential; we shall need to synchronise the occupation of the village with the arrival of the boat; but that should present no great difficulty.'

'And the money?'

'The money will be paid to you as soon as the goods have been delivered.'

'In American dollars?'

'In American dollars,' Lecaros said; and for some reason he smiled faintly, as though the idea of paying in American dollars amused him. 'Are you satisfied?'

Blade wondered about that smile; wondered why a matter of one million, one thousand and eight hundred dollars should be cause for amusement to anyone when they happened to be on the paying end. But it was not important.

'I shall be satisfied when the job is finished,' he said.

Lecaros nodded. 'That is as one would expect. Now to the details.'

For an hour they discussed arrangements. Blade was finally convinced that nothing had been overlooked, and he gave Diego Saurez most of the credit for this; before the conference was finished he had acquired considerable respect for Saurez's intelligence; it was not difficult to see that, though Lecaros might be the leader of the revolutionary movement, Saurez's was surely the brain that planned its strategy.

Eventually there remained only one unsolved problem. Blade himself put it in words.

'How do I get out of the country?' Lecaros appeared surprised at the question. 'The same way as you came in.'

'Is that possible now?'

'Why should it not be possible?'

'There was some trouble on the way here. Haven't you heard?'

'Trouble?' Lecaros said; and he glanced at Lucia. It was obvious that he had not heard. Blade had had an idea that Pedro might have told him; but if it came to the point Pedro knew very little himself; Lucia had not taken him into her confidence regarding the incidents in Nuevo San Tomas.

Now she said, speaking rather hurriedly: 'Father Rubello was arrested. Señor Blade and I were almost taken by the police.'

'Father Rubello arrested!' Lecaros said. 'For what reason?'

'I don't know,' the girl said.

Lecaros shifted his gaze to Blade's face. 'Have you any idea why they should have taken him?'

'Perhaps they discovered his connection with your revolutionary movement.'

'That is unlikely.'

'Then perhaps it was because of the other incident.'

They all looked at him.

'What other incident?' Lecaros asked.

Blade told him about the two bandits, the motor-cycle policeman and the bullet gouge in the Volkswagen.

'I think the man was suspicious. He may have reported the matter and the police may have pulled Father Rubello in after he left me in order to take a closer look at him and the car. Perhaps they didn't care for the sound of his story, and perhaps they found his gun and wondered why it had been fired recently.'

'He could have told them the truth about that.'

'And then they would have wondered why he lied to the man with the motor-cycle. And besides, even if he had told the truth, do you think they would have believed him? A priest with a gun. Wouldn't they be bound to be suspicious and want to find the man who had been with him?'

Lecaros admitted that it seemed likely.

'You didn't tell me this,' Lucia said.

Blade shrugged. 'It didn't seem important.'

'Not important!'

'You knew he had been arrested; you knew the police were looking for me; you had good reason to know that.'

'Nevertheless, you should have told me.'

'Well, if it comes to that,' Blade said, 'there's another little story I didn't tell you either.'

The girl waited. Lecaros and Saurez waited too. Blade let them wait for a few moments; then he said:

'There was trouble in Quintuaquintzl as well. Alvarez killed a man.'

They were startled; he could see that; all of them. But it was Saurez who asked the question.

'Why?'

'The man was a Government agent and he was on my tail. His name was Luis Javado.'

He could see the name meant nothing to them; he had not expected that it would.

'How do you know he was a Government agent?' Lecaros asked.

'He introduced himself to me. He asked a lot of questions, probing questions about my line of business. He called himself a hardware salesman, but he turned up at the Café San Camilo where I had gone to meet Alvarez, and he had a gun. What else could he have been but some kind of security agent?'

'And it was at the Café San Camilo that Alvarez killed him?'

'Yes.'

'Were there any witnesses?'

'Only myself.'

'And the body — what did you do about that?'

'Alvarez made arrangements. He said it would be all right. I hope he was telling the truth, because it could really be awkward if it turned up somewhere.'

'Alvarez is a capable man,' Lecaros said. 'It was an unfortunate complication, but not disastrous.'

'It was for Javado.'

'A man like that is no loss.'

'That, of course, depends on the point of view. Some people might think differently.'

'Perhaps. But I don't see that all this alters the situation. The police have nothing on you; there is nothing with which you can be charged. You will have no difficulty in leaving the country, I am sure.'

'I wish I could share your confidence,' Blade said. 'But frankly I wouldn't say it was beyond their ingenuity to think up some charge on which to pull me in.'

Lucia was looking worried. What Blade had told them seemed to bother her more than it apparently bothered Lecaros. She said thoughtfully:

'I am inclined to agree. There is certainly danger. What do you think, Diego?'

Saurez also seemed disinclined to brush the risk aside as lightly as Lecaros had done. 'It would certainly be unfortunate,' he said, 'if Señor Blade were to be arrested. It is important to us that he gets back to England without delay. He would be of no use to us locked away in a prison cell.'

'You bet your sweet life I wouldn't,' Blade said. 'And if you'll pardon my saying so, I wouldn't want to be shut up in any stinking gaol even if it made no difference whatever to your chances of getting the arms you so badly need. I just happen to prefer being at liberty. Maybe I'm selfish, but that's the way it is.'

Lecaros appeared to be amused by this statement. He grinned at Blade. 'You don't have a taste for martyrdom?'

Blade shook his head. 'It's not my line. So now do you think you could come up with some alternative suggestion for getting me out of the country?'

Saurez had given no sign of sharing Lecaros's amusement; for him it was too serious a matter for joking. 'There are ways and means,' he said. 'It could probably be arranged. These things cost money, of course, but there is a lot at stake.' He turned to Lecaros, questioning him with a glance.

Lecaros nodded, 'Perhaps it would be best.'

Blade noticed an expression of relief on the girl's face. She must really have been worried by the possibility of his being arrested. He wondered whether it was concern for his welfare that had been bothering her or merely the risk of losing the arms shipment. He would have liked to think he mattered more to her than the cause, but he doubted it.

## Chapter Eleven – The Room

It was a green Ford and Lucia was driving. She had picked it up in Nuevo San Tomas at a house on the outskirts of the town. They had arrived in Nuevo San Tomas after nightfall with Pedro in the canoe. Pedro had turned the canoe after landing them and had been swallowed up almost immediately by the darkness. They had gone straight to the house, and a man with a scarred face had let them have the car. Lucia was apparently known to him and he had asked no questions. They had set out at once on the journey to Quintuaquintzl.

'I just hope we don't run into that policeman on the motorcycle,' Blade said. 'The one who questioned Father Rubello. He might remember my face.'

'I'm not planning to run into any policemen,' the girl said.

'But things don't always go according to plan.'

'Now you're being pessimistic again.'

'I'm in a pessimistic frame of mind. I feel tired and dirty, and I can see all sorts of things that could go wrong.'

'There are always things that could go wrong. You just have to make sure they don't.'

'It's as simple as that?'

'It's as simple as that,' she said.

She handled the car well; he had to give her that. One way and another, she was a pretty capable girl, as well as having all those other attributes which had made the few days at the village an all-too-brief delight.

The car surged on through the darkness along the road which he had travelled with Father Rubello in the white Volkswagen, and he sat watching the dim outline of her face and wondering what she would say if he asked her to come to England with him when the job was finished, to share ten thousand pounds and whatever prospects he had in life. But he did not ask her; it was not time yet; the ten thousand pounds were not in his pocket and there were lots of ways they might never be; too many ways. And maybe, too, he was afraid of what her answer might be and wanted to leave it open for a while longer, because it was better to keep the dream alive than to have it shattered by a word.

'You're very silent,' she remarked suddenly. 'What are you thinking about?'

'You,' he said. 'Always you.'

'And does it please you to do that?'

'It pleases me,' Blade said. 'Does it please you to know I'm thinking about you, Lucia?'

'It please me, Francisco.'

It was in his mind to ask her then; the question was almost on his tongue, but he did not give it words. Leave it, leave it. It was not yet time, and he feared the answer, the wrong answer. Instead he asked a different question.

'Do you think you'll be able to contact Alvarez when we get to Quintuaquintzl?'

'I hope so.'

'And if not?'

'I shall have to think of something else.'

He left it at that and fell silent again, just watching her and thinking. He dozed briefly and woke with a start to the sound of the car engine and the white beam of the headlights cutting a swathe through the darkness and throwing into stark relief the imperfections in the road. He stirred and yawned.

'So you are awake again,' she said. 'Do you feel refreshed?'

He felt about as refreshed as a stale bun and his mouth was scummy. 'I never did think going to sleep in cars did anyone much good.'

'And that,' she said, 'is especially so when the anyone happens to be driving.'

'And speaking of driving, would you like me to give you a rest?'

He saw her head turn as she glanced in his direction. 'Are you a good driver?'

'Everyone is a good driver — in his own estimation; didn't you know that? I think I can manage.'

'Leave it until we're through Esperanza,' she said. 'Then you can take over for a while.'

'You're the one that's giving the orders.'

\*

It was a little after midnight when they reached Esperanza, and it was as it had been when Blade had seen it first time from the front seat of

Alvarez's convertible — dead and deserted. Lucia slowed the car but did not stop. A dog slunk away down a side-street as they approached; it was all the life they saw. A mile beyond the town she pulled the car to a halt and they changed seats.

'In England,' Blade said, 'we still drive on the left-hand side of the road.'

'You'd better not try it here,' she told him. 'It could land you in trouble.'

'I'll remember that.'

'And Francisco.'

'Yes, Lucia?'

'Be careful.'

'I'm always careful,' Blade said.

Two minutes later he glanced at her and saw that she was asleep. He hoped she would wake up feeling more refreshed than he had.

There was scarcely any traffic, a few heavy lorries and that was all; no other cars, no police. He was glad about the police; he hoped they were all safely tucked up in bed, or playing cards, or getting up to date with the paper work, anything rather than prowling the roads in patrol cars or setting up checkpoints at strategic places; the last thing he wanted was to run into one of those. But there was nothing to worry about, except maybe the possibility of falling asleep at the wheel from the sheer monotony of it all. As a way of combating this inclination he turned his thoughts to the problem of getting across the border without being arrested, and that kept him awake all right, because it really bothered him; it bothered him more than a little.

The girl appeared to be sleeping sweetly, not stirring, not making a sound. If she had any worries, any misgivings, they were certainly not robbing her of her rest. And yet one might have imagined that she would have been in a state of high nervous tension for the greater part of the time, seeing what kind of business she was engaged in and the dangers involved. So maybe she had just learnt to live with it, the way people learned to live under the perpetual threat of volcanic eruptions and earthquakes and hurricanes.

She was still sleeping when they came to within about five kilometres of Quintuaquintzl, but she woke immediately when he stopped the car. It was as dark as ever, but dawn could not be far away.

'You've had a good sleep,' he said. 'How do you feel after it?'

'I feel fine.' She peered out of the side window. 'Where are we?'

'Not far from Quintuaquintzl. I thought you'd want to take over for the run in.'

'It would be best. You've done very well.'

'I told you I was a good driver.'

'And you kept to the right side of the road?'

'All the way.'

She leaned over and kissed him. 'That's my Francisco.' She stroked his cheek with her fingers. 'And needing a shave again.'

Blade laughed. 'You don't miss a thing, do you?'

They changed places again and she got the car moving, but a little further on she took it down a side-road and brought it to a halt in the shelter of a belt of trees. She switched off the ignition and the lights.

'Why have you stopped here?' Blade asked.

He could see nothing of her but the haziest outline in the darkness, but he heard her turn on the seat.

'It would be rather pointless to drive into the town at this time in the morning. It would be very conspicuous if there were any police to see us, and what could we do? We would have to park somewhere and wait for daylight. It will be better to wait here and go in when the place has come to life.'

It sounded sensible; they would not be so noticeable if they could mingle with the daytime traffic.

'And then?'

'Then I must find Alvarez.'

'Do I come with you?'

'No; I think that would not be wise. You had better get a room. It may take a day, possibly two days, to arrange matters, and you must have somewhere to stay.'

'It had better not be the Hotel Segovia. I'm known there and I don't think the clerk can be trusted.'

She agreed. 'Certainly not the Hotel Segovia. Somewhere of a rather lower class perhaps. You don't mind?'

'I'm not fussy about the standard of the accommodation. Do you know of something suitable?'

'I think so,' she said. 'Something very suitable.'

There was a light breeze blowing; he could hear it whining faintly like a discontented ghost. The stars were partly obscured but there was no rain.

He heard Lucia's voice again, coming with a soft insinuation out of the darkness.

'And now, since we have some time to kill, Francisco mio — and always supposing you do not wish to sleep — perhaps —'

Blade laughed, also very softly. 'Why should I wish to sleep? A man may sleep any time.'

*

'I know this place,' he said. 'I have been here before.'

It was the Café San Camilo.

'Yes,' Lucia said. 'I know.'

She had stopped the car out of sight of the café and they had walked the last part of the way, Blade carrying his bag in his hand, not realising where she was taking him until they were at the door. It was ten o'clock in the morning and the sun was shining.

'But this is where it happened — where Javado was killed.'

'I know that also. You told us.'

'And yet you're suggesting I should lodge here?'

'Have you any objection?'

'Well, of course I have. It would be crazy to put up at the very place where the murder was committed. The police —'

'Why should you imagine the police will be looking here for the murderer? Why should they even be looking for a murderer at all? Didn't you say that Alvarez arranged for the body to be disposed of?'

'Yes, but —'

'If you wish,' she said, 'I will go in first and make sure that everything is all right. You can stay outside until I give you the signal. Do you agree?'

He was not very keen on the idea; he would rather have found some other place to lodge. But there was logic in what she had said; he would probably be as safe at the Café San Camilo as anywhere else. And since the proprietor seemed to have some kind of understanding with Alvarez, and possibly with the girl also, it was unlikely that there would be any treachery there.

He agreed reluctantly. 'But be quick about it. I don't fancy hanging around here. I feel too conspicuous.'

She was gone before he had finished speaking. He walked a little way up the narrow street, feeling that he was being watched from all the windows and doorways. There were a few pedestrians about, and halfway up the hill some kids were playing with a scraggy dog. A broken-down lorry was parked with the tail-board down and two men were lifting an iron boiler on to it. He turned and strolled back again the way he had come.

He was about twenty paces from the Café San Camilo when she came out. She beckoned to him and he smartened his pace.

'It's all right,' she said when he came up to her. 'There's a room you can have.'

'And they haven't had any trouble with the police?'

'No. No trouble at all. You don't have to worry about that Javado business.'

'No? Well, that's nice to know.'

'Come along then. There's no point in standing here.'

She led the way and he followed her inside. The Café San Camilo was not as busy as it had been on the occasion of his previous visit; in fact it was doing very little business at all. There were two old men at a corner table playing draughts or a similar kind of game, there were three other old men reading newspapers, and there was one who was simply staring morosely at an empty cup on the table in front of him. That appeared to be the extent of the clientele at this hour of the day; no doubt things would liven up later, but at the moment the place was certainly not making much profit.

There was only the stout, greasy-haired proprietor behind the bar, and he was wearing a slightly cleaner apron than the one he had had on when Blade had last seen him; but possibly it would become grimier as the day progressed. He seemed none too pleased to see his prospective lodger; possibly he was remembering what had happened the last time Blade had honoured the café with his custom, and was reflecting that something of the kind might happen again. Nevertheless, he came out from behind the bar and made a gesture with his hand to indicate that the other two should follow him. He pushed open the door at the back of the café and went through into the passageway, which was just about as gloomy in the daytime as it had been at night. Then, without as much as a backward glance to see whether they were still with him, he walked to the stairs and began to ascend to the upper floor.

Even before they got there Blade had a feeling that it would be the same room. The floor had been scrubbed, but he could see where the blood had stained the boards. The curtain was drawn back from the window and the daylight seemed to make the room even less attractive than it had appeared when illuminated by a single electric bulb; the blemishes were more apparent, revealed in all their stark repulsiveness; nothing was hidden. But it was that faint stain on the floor that repelled him most; he remembered Javado lying there with the knife in his side, and the hot, stuffy atmosphere of the room oppressed him, made him feel physically sick.

'No,' he said. 'Not here. Not this room.'

The greasy-haired man stared at him with distaste and said in a hoarse, surly voice: 'It is the only one. You can take it, señor, or you can leave it. It is all one to me.' He looked as though he would have added: 'And to hell with you!' The comment was in his eyes, and Blade could read it there.

Blade felt a strong inclination to leave it. His bag was still in his hand and he half-turned towards the door, but the girl put a hand on his arm.

'It will not be for long, and to find some other accommodation would take time and might be difficult. I think you should stay here; it will be safer.'

Blade looked at the greasy-haired man and thought, as he had on first seeing him, that here was someone he could instinctively distrust. This fellow did not strike him as being above a bit of treachery if it happened to be to his advantage. But perhaps in this case treachery would not be to his advantage; after all, there was the matter of Javado, which would not be easy to explain away; the killing had taken place on his premises and he had undoubtedly been implicated. Therefore, if only for his own sake, he had to be trustworthy.

'Please,' Lucia said. 'Please, Francisco.'

Blade set his bag down on the floor, avoiding the patch where Javado had lain. 'Very well, if you say so. I suppose I can endure it for a time. But don't make it too long.'

'It will not be long, I promise you. And while you are here I think it would be advisable if you did not go out. It would be best if you are seen as little as possible.'

'You mean you want me to stay in here?' Blade made a sweeping movement with his arm to indicate the seedy room. 'In this box.'

'There is nothing you need to go out for.'

'Have you forgotten food?'

'Alberto will bring it to you here.'

Blade glanced at Alberto and got the impression that the man was none too pleased to have this task thrust upon him. But he said nothing, accepting the imposition with no more than a shrug of resignation.

'I could eat in the café,' Blade said.

The girl shook her head. 'People might take notice. Why run an unnecessary risk?'

'So,' Blade said, 'I just wait here until you come back. Is that it?'

Again she shook her head. 'I shall not come back. It will be Alvarez. As soon as I have contacted him I shall take the car back to Nuevo San Tomas.'

'And after that?'

'I shall rejoin Raimundo and the others.'

He had a sense of depression; he had not foreseen that she would be leaving immediately; he had imagined that she would return to the café, either alone or with Alvarez. But apparently it was not to be so.

'So I shall not see you again?'

'Who knows, Francisco?'

There was so much he wanted to say to her before she left, so much that he could not say, not with Alberto standing there, stony-faced, oblivious of the fact that he was in the way, and maybe not giving a damn if he was.

Blade gripped the girl's arm and drew her away to the other side of the room. He lowered his voice so that Alberto should not hear.

'You can't walk out on me just like this. I must see you again. Do you want it to end like this?'

'It has to end some time,' she said; but he thought she sounded a little sad about it, as though she too regretted the fact that it must. 'It could not go on for ever.'

He wanted to argue about that, to tell her that he did not agree. He thought of asking the question now, the question he had postponed asking in the car; but there was that damned Alberto still standing by the door, waiting, listening. How in hell was it possible to talk about such matters with that man perhaps overhearing what was said?

'But anyway,' Lucia said, 'we may well see each other again before long, you know.'

'Where? When?'

'You will come back, will you not?'

For the moment that obvious fact had slipped his mind. But of course he had to return; the transaction was not yet completed; the goods had to be delivered and payment collected. His job was far from finished; the ten thousand pounds had yet to be earned.

'And you will be there when I do?'

'Yes,' she said; 'I shall be there.'

Alberto was showing signs of impatience. Blade saw no reason why he had to stay there; but he did, impatient or not.

'I must go now,' Lucia said.

She turned abruptly away from Blade and walked to the door. He watched her go out of the room, but she did not glance back. Alberto followed her and closed the door behind him. Blade half-expected the key to turn in the lock; he had the feeling of being a prisoner. But the key was on the inside of the door; he was free to go if he wished; the only restraint on his movements was the girl's warning that he would be safer where he was.

He crossed to the window and looked out. The room was at the rear of the building and there was a view of a stretch of waste ground, parched and barren, with some houses on the other side, about fifty yards away. Half a dozen boys were kicking an empty tin can that served as a football, and the sound of their voices came to him thinly, like the discordant crying of distant seagulls. He saw a man staring up at the window, and instinctively he drew back out of sight. He had no reason to suppose that the man was anything more than a curious idler, but one could never tell; it would be wiser to keep away from the window.

He lay down on the bed and it creaked in protest. A faintly unpleasant odour rose from the grey blankets, but he ignored it. He stared up at the ceiling and counted the cracks in the plaster. He tried not to look at the place where Javado had dripped his life's blood on to the bare boards of the floor, but his eyes seemed drawn to it against his will. He imagined he could see Javado lying there, twitching slightly. He felt the air pressing upon him like a hot, restricting garment, and there was a filthy taste in his mouth.

He hoped Lucia would find Alvarez quickly and that Alvarez would make the arrangements without delay. He wanted to be gone from there.

## Chapter Twelve – A Word With Captain Varco

It was the woman who brought him a meal. She was no more friendly than the man. Blade had the impression that nothing would have pleased her more than to see the back of him. Since there was no table, she set the tray down on the bed. When he thanked her she answered with a disdainful sniff, as though to say that she could manage very well without his thanks. She turned and left the room, exuding disapproval from every pore.

She returned half an hour later to collect the tray. Blade thanked her again and complimented her on the excellence of the food. It had been far from excellent, but he felt that a little flattery would do no harm and might possibly sweeten relations between them.

'You are the cook, Señora?'

She spoke for the first time, uttering one word only.

'Yes.'

'And a very good one. You have had much experience, no doubt.'

She seemed to relent a little; evidently she was not altogether impervious to flattery. Her shoulders moved slightly under the white blouse she was wearing as though to repudiate any claim to great culinary skill.

'One does what one can.'

'But not everyone could do it so well.'

'If you say so, Señor.'

She went away more kindly disposed towards him, he would have said, than she had been when she came in. It was not important, of course, but her friendship was preferable to her enmity.

There was a dingy little room at the end of the passage which contained an odorous lavatory bowl and a rusty cistern operated by a broken chain, a grimy wash-basin and an undersized bath with yellow rust-streaks under the taps. There was scarcely space to turn round without knocking one's elbows, and there was no detectable difference in the temperature of the water which came from the cold tap and that which came from the hot; it was all tepid and slightly discoloured, as though it had already been used.

Blade washed and shaved, and felt only marginally refreshed by the exercise. He went back to his room and sat on the bed and stared at the place on the floor where Javado had died. He told himself it would not do; it was becoming an obsession; he had better get Javado out of his mind. But that was not easy; the man had a way of slipping back in like an unwelcome guest; his ghostly presence seemed to pervade that wretched room, refusing to go away. Blade wished he had a book to read, something to occupy his brain, but he had nothing. He had given up smoking years ago and could not pass the time by sucking at a cigarette. The minutes passed very slowly, the hours more slowly still. He toyed with the idea of going down to the café and sitting over a drink, but decided not to take the risk of making himself conspicuous. He was glad when the woman brought another meal.

'What is your name?' he asked.

She answered grudgingly, as though parting with something of value: 'Maria.'

'A charming name,' Blade said, wondering just how many of the women in that country shared the same name.

There was nothing else about the woman that could have been called charming: her hair was coarse, her features heavy, her body had thrown off all control and was bulging out in every direction, she had lost two front teeth and had not had them replaced, her ankles were thick and dropsical. And yet he wished to keep her there, that she might drive away by her presence the ghost of the dead man, of Luis Javado whose blood had soaked into the wormy boards.

But she would not stay. She was uneasy; he saw her glance stray to the floor and he wondered whether it was she who had scrubbed away the blood. She turned and walked out of the room, leaving him to entertain Javado alone.

When it grew dark he could stand it no longer; he had to get out of the room, had to breathe some fresh air. And surely it would be safe enough; no one was likely to recognise him; indeed, it would probably have been safe even in the daytime, for who in Quintuaquintzl knew him by sight? Alberto and Maria, the desk clerk at the Hotel Segovia, that was all. And he would certainly not go to the Segovia.

He went down the creaking stairs and out through the café. Alberto, from his position behind the bar, shot a questioning glance at him and seemed to have half a mind to say something, but he gave a shrug and remained silent. No one else appeared to take the slightest notice as he crossed to the door and stepped out into the narrow street.

The air outside was certainly fresher, though still warm. He turned to the right and started to climb the slope, passing the place where the lorry had stood earlier in the day and where the kids had been playing. There were no kids there now and no lorry either. The lighting was poor and he kept a wary eye on the shadowy doorways and gloomy alleys which opened on to the street and in which a man could easily have been lurking. There were probably plenty of characters in this part of the town who would have been only too willing to take an unsuspecting victim by the throat and empty his pockets for him.

But he reached the top of the hill without molestation and turned left into a wider street and walked on, taking little note of where he was going but glad simply to be away from the confining walls of that oppressive room at the Café San Camilo. If he had been more observant regarding the direction in which he was walking he might have avoided the Plaza Hernando Cortez; as it was he came upon the Plaza almost unawares and did not realise just where he was until he saw the shadowy statue of the horse and rider looming over him. He was gazing up at it when he heard the rattle of the trolley-wheels and the whining voice of the legless beggar.

'Señor, for the love of God!'

The man had appeared so swiftly out of the shadows that there had been no chance of evading him except by immediate flight. Blade had no desire to speak to the cripple, but he could not bring himself to turn his back on this unhappy creature. He looked down and saw instant recognition in the man's face.

'Ah, so it is you, señor. You have returned.'

Blade remembered that he had counted three people in Quintuaquintzl who knew him. Perhaps he should have added a fourth, for here was one who knew him by sight if not by name. And Alvarez had warned him about such men as this.

The beggar lifted his cupped hands in supplication. 'Be generous, señor, to one less fortunate than yourself, to one who has no means of living but this.'

'I have given you money twice already,' Blade said.

'True, true. For which I am sincerely grateful; for which I thank your excellency with all my heart.' There was an unmistakably sardonic note in the whining voice. 'But you are rich and I am poor. What are a few pesos to you?'

'What makes you think I am rich?'

'Are not all Americanos rich, señor?'

'I am not Americano.'

'No? Then you are Inglés maybe.'

The man was shrewd; too shrewd perhaps. Blade decided to get away from him. He pulled some money from his pocket and gave it to the beggar.

'I am not rich,' he said. 'But take this.'

The beggar took it. He said: 'You have all your limbs, señor. You have good health also, no doubt. You are indeed rich, believe me.'

Blade walked away, but the voice followed him. 'Take care, Señor. You also could lose your limbs, your health. You also could become a beggar. No man is safe. Take care; take care.'

The voice stopped abruptly and another sound took its place: laughter. The laughter seemed to mock him, to taunt him with that threat of mutilation and penury. The derisive sound of it echoed in his ears even after he could no longer hear it. He had a feeling that he might have done better to have stayed in his room in spite of everything.

*

It was a loud knocking on the door that woke him. He had been having a dream in which Lucia, Father Rubello, Lecaros, Saurez, Pedro, Alberto, Maria, the legless beggar, the clerk at the Hotel Segovia, Korvan and Dancey and the bloodstained corpse of Luis Javado were all inextricably interwoven, and the knocking had at first seemed to be part of the dream; but then the dream faded and the knocking persisted; it at least was real and not imaginary.

The room was in darkness. He looked at the luminous dial of his watch and the time appeared to be nearly two o'clock. Surely Alvarez would not come for him at such an hour in the morning.

The knocking continued. He got out of bed, switched on the light and walked to the door.

'What is it? Who is there?'

He got an answer quickly enough, even if it was not one he would have desired.

'Police! Open up!'

It would have been useless to refuse; they would have forced their way in. He turned the key in the lock and pulled the door open. There were two of them, in uniform, solid men, not well-shaved, armed. Alberto and Maria were hovering uncertainly on the landing behind them, half-dressed looking scared.

'What is this all about?' Blade demanded. But he had a feeling that he knew.

They walked into the room, driving him before them. One of them, the older of the two, said brusquely:

'You are Señor Blade?'

'I am.'

'We must ask you to come with us to headquarters. You will please get dressed.'

'Why?'

'Orders. You are required for questioning.'

'Questioning? In connection with what?'

'You will be told when you get there. Now please get dressed.'

'Can't it wait until morning?'

'No.'

'But this is ridiculous. You must tell me why I am wanted for questioning. Have you a warrant to arrest me?'

The younger policeman gave a faint smile. The other man remained stolid, unmoved.

'If you refuse to dress we shall be forced to take you as you are. The choice is yours.'

Blade decided to get dressed. The two policemen watched him. Alberto and Maria watched from the door. He could not remember when he had had such an audience to see him putting on his clothes.

There was a jeep standing outside the café. The younger policeman drove. It was not far. Police headquarters was a plain square building of white stone, glimmering palely in the artificial light. Blade was taken inside and conducted to a room where a man of about forty was sitting at a desk cluttered with papers, a pile of manila folders on his right. He looked sleepy and, like the policemen, was in need of a shave. He introduced himself as Captain Varco and invited Blade to sit down.

There was a chair in front of the desk and Blade sat down on it, facing Captain Varco, who dismissed the two policemen with a gesture of the hand. They went out of the room and closed the door behind them.

'You are wondering no doubt why you have been brought here, Señor Blade,' Captain Varco said. He had a pleasant voice, warm and friendly; he gave the impression of being a warm and friendly person; a kind of human spaniel.

Blade confirmed that he was indeed wondering.

'And perhaps you resent being dragged out of bed? You were in bed?'

'Yes.'

Captain Varco stifled a yawn with his hand and smiled apologetically. 'I myself have not even been to bed. Duty. It is a hard taskmaster. So you decided to come back to Quintuaquintzl, Señor Blade.'

'To come back?'

'You have been here before, I believe. Not many days ago. At the Hotel Segovia. That is correct?'

'Yes.'

'We rather hoped you would return.'

'Yes?'

'Oh, indeed yes. And then, only a few hours ago, we received information that you had been seen in the town.'

'Is that so?' Blade said; and he thought at once of the legless beggar and remembered Alvarez telling him that the police made use of such men as informers. Certainly he would have been wise to have stayed in his room.

'That is so,' Captain Varco said. 'And then of course we made inquiries at the hotels, and none of them appeared to have anyone of your name or answering your description in residence. Tell me, why didn't you go again to the Hotel Segovia? Were you dissatisfied with the service?'

'No; I wasn't dissatisfied. I just thought I'd like a change.'

'And so you went to the Café San Camilo. Hardly a change for the better, I would have thought.'

'Possibly not.'

'It did not occur to us at first that you might be there. That is why it was so late when my men came for you.'

'So it wasn't done simply to inconvenience me?'

Captain Varco gave a comfortable laugh which seemed to come up from somewhere in the region of his stomach. 'Oh, no. You mustn't imagine we employ those methods. We would have left it until morning, but the matter is of some considerable urgency.'

'What matter?'

'Ah, of course you don't yet know why we wished to question you. Forgive me; I should have told you. It is the affair of Luis Javado.'

'Javado!' Blade said; and he was aware that Varco, for all his appearance of sleepiness, was watching him closely, observing his reaction. 'You mean —'

'I mean the gentleman who was at the Hotel Segovia at the time when you were there. Who, I believe, had some conversation with you. Who even visited you in your room on the very day when you departed so abruptly. Am I correct?'

'Quite correct.'

'Would you mind telling me what you and Señor Javado discussed on those occasions?'

'A variety of matters. I don't remember everything.'

'But something in particular, perhaps?'

'Nothing of importance. He told me he was a travelling salesman, a representative. In the hardware line.'

'What kind of hardware?'

'He didn't say.'

'And you have no idea why he should have wished to talk to you?'

'I imagine he picked me out as someone who would listen to him. I think he just liked to talk, liked to hear the sound of his own voice. The fact is, he was a bore.'

'You found his conversation boring?'

'Very much so.'

Captain Varco shifted the manila folders by about one millimetre, straightened some of the papers, rested his elbows on the desk, made a bridge with his fingers, and asked mildly:

'Why did you leave the Hotel Segovia so suddenly?'

It was a difficult question to answer. Blade sidestepped it.

'Surely that is my business.'

'Your business, yes. But what kind of business, may I ask?'

'Perhaps business would be the wrong word. Recreation might be a better description.'

'So tell me about this recreation.'

'I don't think I should do that.'

Captain Varco raised his eyebrows. 'Why not?'

'There is a lady involved. I doubt whether she would wish to have her name revealed. She is married and it could be compromising, you understand?'

Varco smiled. 'I understand. An affair of the heart. Is that what you are telling me?'

'Yes.'

'And of course the note you received was from this lady?'

'Note?'

'I believe you had a communication while Señor Javado was in your room. After that you left the hotel, returned later, and then checked out. Is that so?'

Blade saw that Varco was very well-informed, and it was not difficult to guess the identity of the informant; it could hardly have been anyone but the hotel clerk.

'Yes,' he said; 'that is so.'

'And the communication was from the lady?'

'Yes.'

Varco nodded thoughtfully. 'Now let us get all this straight. You received the note; you went out to make certain arrangements; you came back to the hotel and checked out. Then you went to join the lady?'

'That's about it.'

'There's nothing else you wish to add? No little extra details perhaps?'

'There's nothing else I can remember. Nothing important.'

Varco allowed the bridge of his fingers to collapse and leaned back in his chair, watching Blade with those apparently sleepy eyes which Blade did not believe were sleepy at all.

'You did not by any chance encounter Señor Javado after he left your room? While you were out making those arrangements, perhaps?'

'No. In fact I have not seen Señor Javado since. He was, after all, no more than a chance acquaintance. We really had nothing in common.'

'I see.'

Captain Varco said nothing more for a while. He closed his eyes and looked as if he had really gone to sleep.

Finally Blade said: 'Is that all?'

Varco seemed to wake with a start. 'Forgive me, Señor Blade. You were saying —?'

'I asked whether that was all. Have you any more questions to put to me?'

'No; no more questions.'

'So I may go back to bed?'

'Certainly. I will have you taken back to the Café San Camilo. I am greatly obliged to you. You have been most co-operative.'

Blade stood up.

Captain Varco put a hand to his head. 'What am I thinking of? There is of course one more question. Who was it who picked you up at the Plaza Hernando Cortez?'

'The Plaza Hernando Cortez?'

'Yes. On the evening when you left the Hotel Segovia you were observed getting into a car which was then driven away — by a man. You said your assignation — if I may call it that — was with a lady. So who was the man?'

Blade saw that the legless beggar must have reported that too. He wondered how much the informer was paid; it would certainly be a useful addition to his income from begging. No wonder there had been that note of mockery in his voice.

Captain Varco was waiting.

'The man,' Blade said, 'was the lady's servant. He had been sent to pick me up.'

Surprisingly, Captain Varco appeared to accept this explanation. 'Ah, of course, of course.'

He got up from his chair, came round to the front of the desk, and ushered Blade to the door. 'I am sorry to have bothered you, but these things —'

'I understand.'

At the door Varco paused, his hand still on Blade's arm. 'There is just one thing that puzzles me,' he said. 'You have not asked me why we are so interested in your relations with Señor Javado. Aren't you at all curious to know?'

'I imagined it was because he has disappeared.'

'Did I tell you he had disappeared?'

'No. But why else would you ask all those questions? I naturally concluded that you must be looking for him.'

'You were wrong, Señor Blade.'

Blade was startled. 'Wrong!'

Captain Varco smiled, and there was nothing friendly or comfortable about this particular smile. It was grim, very grim indeed.

'No; we are certainly not looking for Señor Javado. We know exactly where he is. He is in the mortuary. His body was discovered in a disused quarry five kilometres out of town. He had been stabbed, Señor Blade, stabbed with a knife.'

## Chapter Thirteen – Joe

'You were wrong about those men,' Blade said.

He looked at Alvarez accusingly, blaming him.

'What men?' Alvarez asked.

'Those men who were supposed to deal with Javado's body. You said it would never be found after they had disposed of it. But it was.'

'That was unfortunate,' Alvarez admitted, 'but such things happen.' He did not appear to be greatly concerned. 'It is never possible to guarantee one hundred per cent infallibility.'

It was the morning after Blade's interview with Captain Varco of the Quintuaquintzl Police and they were in the room at the Café San Camilo. Blade had been brought back by the two policemen in the jeep and had gone to bed again, but had found sleep elusive; he had not been sorry when the sun rose and a new day started.

Maria had brought him breakfast but had appeared sullen and disinclined to talk, an expression of dislike amounting almost to hatred imprinted on her heavy features. He could not blame her; in her eyes he must look like someone who brought nothing but trouble to the house; no doubt she would be glad to see the back of him. And if it came to that, he would be glad to be gone.

Alvarez had arrived soon after the meal. The door had not been locked and he had slipped in without knocking. Blade had been pleased to see him; it meant that the waiting was ended.

Alvarez said: 'You should not have gone out last night. You were warned.'

'I got sick of the room. It was playing on my nerves.'

'And now, of course, you have made things a little more difficult.'

'In what way?'

'Go to the window,' Alvarez said. 'Tell me what you can see.'

Blade walked to the window and looked out. There was the patch of waste ground; there were the houses on the opposite side; two or three stray dogs; an old lorry with a man sleeping in the cab; the inevitable kids. He told Alvarez.

'The man is not asleep,' Alvarez said. 'He is keeping watch on the place. He will have seen you at the window. The front of the café is being watched also. There are two agents of the police drinking coffee at one of the tables.'

'You are sure?'

'Alberto is not blind,' Alvarez said. 'And what else would you expect? Did you really imagine that Captain Varco swallowed that story you told him? About the mysterious and captivating lady.'

Blade had to admit to himself that it had been rather too easy. 'But if he didn't accept it, why did he let me go?'

'He knows where you are. He has you safely bottled up. And of course you are not really very important in yourself; he is looking for bigger fish. With your help he hopes to catch them.'

Blade looked into Alvarez's leathery face. 'And you are one of the bigger fish?'

'Perhaps.'

'So how did you get in without being picked up?'

'For one thing,' Alvarez said, 'I am not known to them by sight. And for another thing, I did not come in either by the front or the back entrance.'

'Then how did you come in?'

Alvarez bared his teeth in a sudden unexpected grin. 'The same way by which you and I will get out.'

\*

There was a cellar under the Café San Camilo. There were casks of wine and spirits in the cellar, racks of bottles, nothing apparently out of the ordinary, nothing of which one would take particular notice. At the far end, however, there was a concealed doorway hidden away behind a stack of empty barrels, and on the other side of the doorway was a narrow tunnel. The tunnel ran beneath the street and came out in another cellar under the house on the opposite side. This house had not been lived in for some time and was used as a store for junk. Alvarez said it belonged to a cousin of Alberto's, but the cousin was very seldom there because he was a compulsive gambler and spent most of his time playing cards or shooting craps or attending cockfights. Alvarez said it was rather fortunate that the police knew nothing of the tunnel, since otherwise they might have kept watch on the junk store as well, and that would have made things really very difficult indeed.

# Final Run

The back door of the junk store opened on to a yard with a corrugated-iron fence surrounding it, and there was a lot of junk in the yard as well. Alvarez led the way across the yard and opened a gate which gave access to an alleyway. There was no one in the alleyway, and they walked briskly to the end of it where the black convertible was parked in a cul-de-sac.

'You had it all worked out,' Blade said.

Alvarez unlocked the doors of the convertible. 'Get in,' he said. 'We have no time to lose.'

Blade got in and threw his bag on to the back seat. Alvarez started the engine. There was no sign of any policemen.

\*

They were thirty kilometres out of Quintuaquintzl and Alvarez had been pushing the convertible more than a little. The first flush of elation at having got clear of the town had soon worn off, and Blade was experiencing a certain reaction. Things could still go wrong and he would not feel happy until he was out of the country. Alvarez had spoken very little and it could well have been that he too was feeling slightly tense. They were heading in the direction of the border, but all Blade's efforts to persuade Alvarez to explain just how he intended making the crossing had met with very little result. Alvarez seemed reluctant to talk about it and all he would say was that the arrangements had been made and that there was no need to worry. Blade carried on worrying nevertheless.

They passed a sign which indicated that it was just forty kilometres to La Cruz, and Blade knew that La Cruz was a border town. But he could not think that the crossing was going to be made there; at that kind of place it would be more difficult than anywhere to slip across the frontier undetected; there would be too many checks.

And then, some five kilometres further on, Alvarez turned the car off on to a minor road that was nothing but dust and stones. There were fences on both sides and cultivated ground, men working in fields of maize and cotton and tobacco, and here and there a tractor or lorry.

Alvarez drove for another two or three kilometres along this road, and then slowed and turned left through an open gateway and on to a very rough track indeed which led to a big wooden shed or barn. He took the car round to the other side of the shed, stopped it and got out. Blade got out too, and he could hear the sound of a helicopter not far off. A moment later he spotted it; it was crop-spraying, flying low and coming towards them.

Alvarez stood with his back to the car and waved his arms in a kind of semaphore. The pilot of the helicopter must have spotted him at once, for the machine came nearly up to the shed, hovered a few moments in mid-air and then lowered itself on to a patch of level ground some thirty paces from where the car was parked. The pilot climbed out as the rotor gradually stopped revolving and walked towards the car. He was red-haired, lean and craggy. He greeted Alvarez in Spanish, but Blade could tell that it was not really his language; at a guess he would have said that the man was an American — the northern variety.

'So you got here,' the man said. 'Any trouble?'

'No trouble,' Alvarez said. 'Are you ready?'

'As soon as I've topped up the fuel tank.' He looked at Blade. 'You're the passenger?'

'I'm the passenger,' Blade said.

'I'm Joe,' the red-headed man said. 'I'll get the juice. The sooner we get going, the sooner I'll be back on the legitimate job.'

He went into the shed and came out with two cans of petrol.

Blade turned to Alvarez. 'That's a useful sideline for a crop-sprayer — hopping across the border. Does he do it often?'

'Why don't you ask him?' Alvarez said.

'Maybe I will. And maybe it's the spraying that's really the sideline.'

They watched Joe topping up the tank of the helicopter. There was nobody else in sight, but Alvarez kept glancing towards the road as though afraid there might be somebody on his tail.

'If you're worried,' Blade said, 'why don't you go? There's nothing more for you to do now.'

Alvarez frowned. 'I am not worried. And besides, I have to be sure that you are safely away.'

Worried or not, Blade noticed that he was still keeping a wary eye on the road, possibly looking for a tell-tale cloud of dust. Blade himself was feeling pretty much on edge; he wished the pilot would hurry with the topping-up job, but there was no way of speeding up that kind of operation.

In fact it was finished fairly quickly. Joe took the empty cans into the shed, came out again and said in English:

'Okay. Let's go.'

There was very little spare room in the helicopter; when two people were inside the bubble it was just about full. But there was a good wide view from the cockpit, and as the rotor began to turn Blade caught sight of a cloud of dust on the road. He could see that the dust-cloud was being made by a big car travelling at speed, and he wondered whether Alvarez had spotted it too. He glanced towards the convertible, which was still parked by the shed, and he knew then that Alvarez had indeed seen the other car, because there was a gun in Alvarez's hand.

There was still a chance that the car making the dust-cloud might have nothing to do with them and might in fact be on some quite different business, but when it reached the track leading to the shed it slowed and swung off the road, and he knew that it had a lot to do with them and that Alvarez was going to need his gun.

The rotor was revolving faster now. Blade was not sure whether Joe had seen the approaching car; he might have been too busy with the controls. The helicopter was beginning to lift off when the car skidded to a halt, the doors burst open, and four men spilled out, two in police uniform, two in plain clothes. One of the men in plain clothes was carrying a sub-machine-gun; he raised it to his shoulder, took rapid aim at the rising helicopter and loosed off a burst of fire.

If Joe had been unaware of the newcomers before, he became aware of them then.

'What in hell's going on?' he yelled.

Blade yelled back at him over the racket of the engine and the rotor: 'We're being fired at, that's what.' He wondered just how close the bullets had gone. There was no indication that any of them had hit the target.

'Christ!' Joe said. 'We better get the hell outa here.'

It was the only thing to do. If they went back they could not help Alvarez; Blade had no gun, and if Joe had one it was not likely that he would get the chance to use it. All the same, he felt pretty sick about leaving Alvarez to fight it out by himself.

Not that Alvarez was doing so badly nevertheless. He was crouching down behind the convertible and firing his pistol across the top of the bonnet. He had a good appreciation of the priorities too: Blade saw the man with the submachine-gun suddenly drop the weapon, stagger a pace or two and fall to the ground. Which was one up to Alvarez.

The helicopter was moving away rapidly now; the figures on the ground, the two cars, even the shed, began to dwindle in size as the distance increased, and Blade could no longer see how Alvarez was faring. But there could be only one outcome of so unequal a fight; the odds were too heavily stacked against him; he must eventually be killed or overpowered.

And Blade doubted whether that leathery-faced man would let himself be taken alive; he would fight it out to the end.

Joe seemed to be having similar thoughts. 'A tough old guy, that Alvarez.'

'You've had dealings with him before?'

'Some. Guess there won't be any more dealings of that sort now. Guess I'll never get to finish that spray job neither; they'll have to call in another contractor. Well, that's the way it goes.' He sounded philosophical about it. 'You work up a nice little business and then something comes along to break it up. So then you just have to start up again some place else.'

'You've carried other passengers this way?'

'A few. Other things too. Packages; small size, big value. Get me?'

Blade got him. Joe was in the smuggling line. Maybe he had lifted quite a cargo of drugs in his time. Hot money too? That was a thought. He looked at the red-headed man; at close quarters the American appeared older; there was a network of small creases in the dry skin of his craggy face, and his mouth was hard. He was not likely to lose any sleep over leaving Alvarez to his fate.

'Where are you from, Joe?'

'Dayton, Ohio. You ever been there?'

'No, I've never been there.'

'You didn't miss a lot,' Joe said.

Not long after that he directed Blade's attention to the ground sliding away below them.

'See that river?'

The river was a silver thread winding through the landscape.

'I see it.'

'That's the border,' Joe said. 'You're out.'

## Chapter Fourteen – Word Of Advice

'So you had a little bother,' Korvan said. He drew smoke out of his cigar and watched it drift away from his mouth. 'That was a pity. It should all have gone smoothly.'

Korvan was as neatly parcelled up as ever; he was wearing a dark blue suit which fitted snugly over the shoulders, a plain white shirt, a plain blue tie and plain black shoes, very highly polished. His tightly curled hair was precisely the same length as it always was; Blade had a feeling that it was trimmed daily; perhaps Dancey trimmed it for him, adding that to his other duties.

Dancey was always around; he was Korvan's bodyguard, errand-boy, butt. Korvan treated him with contemptuous familiarity, not giving a damn about Dancey's feelings, not giving a damn whether or not he had any feelings. But Dancey did have feelings, Blade was sure of that, and one day perhaps Korvan would goad him too far. Dancey was a dangerous man; he might not be very bright in the head; if he had been a little brighter he would probably not have stayed with Korvan so long, to be kicked around like a dog, treated as a lackey, used as a doormat. But there were limits, and one day Korvan might overstep those limits and Dancey might react in the one way he knew how to react — with violence. If Blade had been in Korvan's highly-polished shoes he would have been a shade more careful.

'Rather more than a little bother, I'd have called it,' he said. 'Your Central American representative could very well have lost his life. Do you know that?'

Dancey gave his cackling laugh. 'Central American representative! Is that what you call yourself?'

'I was in Central America; I was acting as Mr. Korvan's representative. What would you say that makes me?'

'Don't waste your breath talking to him,' Korvan said. 'He's a pin-brain; you should know that. The odds are he doesn't even know where Central America is.'

Dancey went red in the face, but he said nothing; just stared at Korvan, scowling.

'Look at him,' Korvan said. 'Look at the big baboon. Now he's angry. He gets angry because I tell the truth about him. Some people, they just can't take the truth.'

'Never mind the truth,' Blade said. 'Let's talk about finance, about my ten thousand pounds. When do I get it?'

Korvan answered in that curiously tight-lipped way of his: 'You get the money when you finish the job.'

'I have finished the job. I've got you your order.'

'But you know very well that isn't the whole job. You know there is the other half still to do.'

'What other half?'

'The delivery of the merchandise, of course. And the collection of the dollars. You knew you had to collect. I told you. It was part of the bargain.'

'Things have altered. If I go back there and the security people, the police, get their hands on me I'm really going to be in trouble. I only got away by the skin of my teeth last time. Next time I mightn't be so lucky.'

'You're making too much fuss,' Korvan said. 'You won't be caught. You'll be all right.'

Which was easy enough to say, Blade thought. Sitting there in Korvan's expensively furnished country house, looking out on to lawns and terraces where gardeners were at work with mowers and electric clippers, it might seem like a simple matter to ship a cargo of arms and ammunition to a Central American revolutionary army. At least it might seem like that to Korvan, because he would not be going; he would not even see the cargo; he would just take his profit and not care two pins if some other people burnt their fingers getting it for him.

'I don't want anything more to do with it,' Blade said. 'Send somebody else to collect the cash. Send him.' He pointed a finger at Dancey.

'I told you before,' Korvan said, 'he isn't capable of doing the job. He doesn't have the brains of a louse. He doesn't know the language and I doubt whether he could even count the money.' He glanced at Dancey. 'Could you, you big ape?'

Again Dancey's face darkened. 'I can count. You got no call to talk to me like that. I got brains, too.'

'Now see what I've done,' Korvan said mockingly. 'I've touched him on a tender spot. You wouldn't think he was a sensitive plant, not to look at him. But he is. I think he gets more sensitive every day. Maybe he ought to see a psychiatrist. What do you say, Frank?'

Blade could see Dancey's big fists clenched on his knees as though he would have liked to start hitting out with them. There was a dribble of saliva on Dancey's lower lip and anger in his eyes.

'I say we should get back to the business,' Blade said. 'Do I get my ten thousand quid or don't I?'

'You will get your money when you've brought me —' Korvan consulted a slip of paper with some figures on it — 'a sum of one million, one thousand and eight hundred dollars.'

'You can go to hell,' Blade said.

He got up, walked to the window and stared out at the garden, hands thrust deeply into his trouser-pockets.

Korvan's voice behind him sounded faintly amused. 'You don't mean that, of course. Certainly I may go to hell eventually, but not just yet. And certainly you will go again to Central America and conclude the transaction. You know it, don't you, Frank? This is only play-acting. You know you will go.'

Korvan was right, damn him. Blade did know it. There had never been any question of not going; he had simply been making the gestures of protest. He would go because he needed the money and there was no way on earth of forcing Korvan to cough up without going. And he would go also because he had promised Lucia Mandego that he would: he would go because he wanted to see her again, because he hoped to persuade her to come away with him. Ten thousand pounds was a powerful reason for going, but the other reason was even stronger. He had to go back.

One of the gardeners was fixing up a revolving sprayer to give the lawn a soaking. There had been a spell of dry weather, but Korvan's lawns looked green enough; like everything else connected with the man, they were flourishing. Blade hated Korvan; this dealer in arms who never even saw the merchandise he sold and never came into contact with the people who bought it. What did he know of guerilla fighting? Of that white-hot flame of idealism which made men revolt against an oppressive régime? He was too cold a fish to understand the passions that drove such men and women; would not have understood if it had been explained to him; would not have cared. He was interested only in how much there was in it for him; how many dollars he could extract from this trade in death.

Again Blade heard Korvan's voice, bland and self-satisfied: 'Come away from the window, Frank. Come and sit down again and let's talk some more. Let's get everything straight.'

Blade turned away from the window, walked back to his chair and sat down. Korvan gave a lupine smile.

'That's better. You are going to be sensible, of course. You are going to complete the job.'

'You ought to pay me more,' Blade said; hating Korvan, hating his guts. 'I made a good bargain; I got you more for the goods than the lowest you were prepared to take. I ought to have a percentage of the difference.'

Korvan sucked at his cigar, staring at Blade with those curiously opaque eyes of his, like frosted windows on the soul — if he could have been said to possess a soul.

'I don't recall anything of that kind being mentioned in our agreement. My recollection is that the fee was to be ten thousand pounds, plus legitimate expenses. There was nothing said about commission or anything of that description. You were with us at the time, Dancey. Did you hear me make any offer of commission to our mutual friend?'

'No,' Dancey said, 'I didn't hear nothing.' He sounded bad-tempered, still perhaps smarting under the insults Korvan had heaped upon him. But he was not resentful enough to back Blade against his employer.

'There,' Korvan said. 'You heard what Dancey said. He doesn't recall any agreement along those lines either. What gave you the idea that we had one?'

'You know damn well I didn't say we had,' Blade said. 'So don't pretend I did say that, you bastard. All I said was that I ought to have a percentage of the extra cash I managed to get for you. Hell, I could have told you they beat me down to rock bottom and you would have been none the wiser. I could have pocketed the difference.'

'And why didn't you, Frank?' Korvan still sounded amused; being called a bastard had not bothered him. 'Why didn't you do that?'

'I'm damned if I know.'

'I'll tell you why,' Korvan said. 'Because you're too honest. And that's why I employed you. I told you so, didn't I? I trust you.'

'Maybe you shouldn't push that trust too far. A million dollars is a pretty big temptation.'

'Are you telling me you might take off with the cash?'

'It's a possibility, isn't it? You've got to admit it really is a possibility.'

Blade was aware that another person besides Korvan was watching him closely; the other person was Dancey. He had a feeling that Dancey might be rather pleased if Korvan were to be cheated out of a million dollars.

'You wouldn't do it,' Korvan said.

Blade looked at him coolly. 'Don't bet on that.'

Korvan shook his head; he seemed unbothered. 'You wouldn't do it because you have more sense — quite apart from the fact that you're so honest. You know you wouldn't get away with it.'

'Is that a threat?'

'Call it a friendly word of advice. Let me tell you a little story. Once upon a time there was a man who thought he would double-cross me. You know what happened? He disappeared. Nobody knew where he went; he just vanished, into thin air as they say. But I know where he is. There's a block of flats in Croydon that's got a man's body in the foundations, all nicely wrapped up in concrete. He's safe there. Nobody's going to pull down all those flats and break up the foundations to find him. Think about it, Frank.'

'You'll never wrap me up in concrete,' Blade said.

Korvan smiled. 'I don't want to, Frank; believe me, I don't. But if you should ever get any ideas about taking off with a million dollars of my money, remember that man holding up a block of flats.'

'I'll remember.'

'Of course you will.' Korvan did a little work on the cigar and then gave a laugh. 'But why are we talking like this? It's all nonsense. We know you're only joking. All right then, we've had our bit of fun, so now let's get back to business.'

They got back to business.

## Chapter Fifteen – A Sack Of Money

They went in after dark. There were some lights showing in the fishing village, a shadowy mass of higher ground behind. There had been no trouble. It had all gone according to plan.

Blade had joined the ship in Tangier; it was a motor vessel of rather less than nine hundred gross tons; not very new, not very smart as to paintwork and brass; the kind of ship that could slip into little ports without fuss and discharge a cargo with its own gear. It was registered in Liberia and was owned by a company which Blade had never heard of, but in which he would have been prepared to wager Korvan had a very big finger.

The captain was a man named Svenssen, who looked like a pirate and probably had Viking blood in him. He could not have been more than thirty but he was a hard case sure enough, and he needed to be; he had a whole crew of hard cases to keep under control.

Blade disliked Svenssen on sight; there was too much swagger to the man. He was well over six feet tall and must have weighed at least sixteen stone. And it was all bone and muscle, no fat. He really was hard. Blade saw him once strike a seaman with his fist for being insolent. It knocked the man cold. Not that anyone seemed to think it was anything out of the ordinary; that was the kind of ship it was.

Blade was on the bridge when they went in. They had exchanged signals with the shore and everything seemed to be all right, but he felt edgy nevertheless; things might yet go wrong and he could not forget that in this country he was a wanted man. He would be thankful when they had dumped the cargo and were away again.

Svenssen seemed cool enough; it was certainly not the first time he had taken part in this kind of operation, and maybe it would not be the last.

'Nice little harbour,' he said. He sounded like a connoisseur of nice little harbours. 'Cosy. You think so, huh?'

'Very cosy,' Blade said, just to humour Svenssen; but he was damned if he could see anything cosy about it.

There was a stone quay, and there were two or three small fishing-boats huddled against it; but there was a berth for the ship and Svenssen brought

# Final Run

it up to the quay so gently there was scarcely a tremor as the hull made contact. Some shadowy figures took the mooring-ropes and slipped them over the bollards. Other shadowy figures were moving around, and Blade saw that they were carrying guns. He hoped they were Lecaros's men.

Two minutes later any misgivings he might have had on that score were put at rest. Lecaros himself was on board, and so also were Diego Saurez and Lucia Mandego.

*

They talked in the saloon. From outside they could hear the sound of winches and men shouting orders as the cargo came up from the holds. There was no time to lose; they wanted it all to be ashore by daylight, and that meant working at full stretch throughout the night.

'So, Señor Blade,' Lecaros said, 'you had some trouble getting away.'

'You heard about that?'

'I heard about it.'

'And Alvarez?'

'He is dead, of course.'

'I'm sorry,' Blade said. He had known it must end like that; there had been no way Alvarez could have escaped except by a miracle; and miracles just did not happen. 'I'm sorry.'

Lecaros shrugged. 'Such things cannot always be avoided; it is the fortune of war.' He gave Blade a keen look. 'You are not blaming yourself because you got away and Alvarez died? That would be foolish. What could you have done? I will tell you; you could have got yourself killed also. And how would that have helped anyone?'

'If it comes to that, I had no choice anyway,' Blade said. 'The helicopter was already taking off and the pilot wouldn't have gone back; he was too concerned for his own skin.'

'That is understandable.'

'And Father Rubello? Have you heard anything of him?'

It was Lucia who answered. 'Father Rubello has been released. There was no charge they could make against him.'

'There was the gun.'

'In this country it is not a crime to carry a gun — even for a priest.'

'So they didn't get him to talk?'

'No.'

'That's one tough little priest,' Blade said. 'I'm glad they let him go.'

'Though of course,' Lecaros said, 'he is no longer of any use to us.'

'Why not?'

'Because they will watch him like hawks. It is perhaps why they released him.'

'Yes, I suppose so,' Blade said. 'You heard that the police picked me up in Quintuaquintzl?'

Lecaros nodded. 'We heard that.' They seemed to hear most things; it looked as though the grapevine was in good working order.

'You should have stayed in your room,' Lucia said. 'I warned you.'

'I know you warned me, but I got sick of Javado for company.'

'Javado!' Lecaros said sharply. 'How could he —?'

'It was the room he died in. There was a bloodstain on the floor. He kept coming back every time I closed my eyes.'

'You are too imaginative. A dead man is dead. There is no return.'

'Well, maybe not, but that's the way it seemed. Have you brought the money?'

'It is here,' Saurez said. He pointed at a small coarse sack which he had carried in and dumped on the floor of the saloon. 'All of it.'

'Well, I'll be hanged!' Blade stared at the container. 'You mean to say that's really it? Do you know this is the first time I've ever seen a sack of money?'

Saurez appeared unimpressed by this revelation. 'You had better count it,' he said.

'Yes, I'd better do that. But not in here.'

'Why not? What is wrong with this room?'

'It's a shade too public; anyone could walk in,' Blade said. He was thinking especially of Svenssen, but he would have been reluctant to let any member of the ship's company get a sight of the money. None of them knew he was collecting cash for the arms, and the longer they remained in ignorance of that fact the better it would be. There was not one of them he would have trusted with his wrist-watch, let alone a million and more dollars; and that went for Svenssen as much as anybody.

Lecaros appeared to understand. 'So where do you propose to count it?'

'In my cabin.'

'Someone should go with you — as a witness.'

Blade grinned. 'You're thinking I might slip a few dollars under the mattress and swear you'd given short weight, is that it? Don't you trust me?'

'I trust you,' Lecaros said; 'but for your own sake I think there should be a witness.'

'All right, but only one. It's a small cabin and more than that would be a crowd.'

'I'll go with you,' Lucia said.

Blade nodded. 'That suits me.' He picked up the sack. 'Let's go then.'

The cabin was certainly small; the bunk took up nearly half the space and there was only just room for a narrow wardrobe, a wash-basin and a chair. Blade locked the door and drew a curtain across the single porthole. He loosed the cord securing the mouth of the sack and tipped the contents on to the bunk. Then he stood perfectly still for a few moments, just letting his eyes get used to the sight of so much money.

'My!' he whispered. 'My, oh my!'

They were all new one-hundred-dollar bills. They were made up into bundles and there were a lot of bundles, a hell of a lot.

'Well?' the girl said. 'Are you going to count them, or are you just going to stand there gaping at them? Haven't you seen money before?'

Blade shook his head. 'Not this kind of money. Not all in one heap. He must have robbed a bank.'

Lucia gave a laugh. 'Yes, of course. What else? An American bank.'

'Chase Manhattan or First National?' Blade asked. But he was not so sure she was joking. How the devil did Lecaros and his crowd get possession of a million dollars in brand new one-hundred-dollar bills? It could hardly have been by honest means. Well, that was not his worry; let Korvan work that one out. He sat down on the end of the bunk and began to count the money.

It was all there, down to the last hundred dollars. He had heard the expression, a cool million, and here it was, as cool as they came; a cool million and another eighteen hundred on top for good measure.

Lucia was looking at him. 'Satisfied?'

'I'm satisfied that the amount is correct.'

She held the sack open for him while he put the money back where it had come from. He tied the cord and pushed the sack under his bunk.

There was a sudden crackle of machine-gun fire and he stiffened.

'What the —'

Lucia said calmly: 'Don't be alarmed. They're simply testing the wares. You didn't expect us to take things on trust, did you? Your Mr. Korvan might have done a crooked deal. We should hate to be left with a lot of useless rubbish.'

'You think Korvan would do a thing like that?'

'Don't you?'

Blade thought it highly likely that Korvan might do a thing like that if he thought he could get away with it. He would certainly not be above packing the crates with rocks or old iron and topping up with a few genuine guns for camouflage; that way the profit would be a lot higher. Not that Korvan himself had done any of the packing, of course; but that was not to say that he had not instructed his agents to do it that way. Blade could not avoid a faint sense of uneasiness, because he was the man on the spot, and if Lecaros found any rubbish in the consignment he was the one who was going to be asked for an explanation. And that kind of thing was not a matter that would be easy to explain in any very satisfactory fashion.

There was another burst of firing. He recognised the distinctive sound of a high-velocity rifle.

'Are they going to test every weapon?'

'I don't think that's likely,' the girl said. 'They'll just take a sample here and there; not necessarily from the top of the pack.'

They could hear the muffled sounds of activity on deck as the unloading of the cargo proceeded.

'The people in the village — did they give you any trouble?'

'None at all,' Lucia said. 'What could they have done against so many armed men, even if they had wished to do anything? And in their hearts they are on our side.'

It was hot in the cabin. Blade was sweating a little.

'I want you to come with me,' he said.

She looked puzzled. 'Go with you? Where?'

'To England.'

'You're joking,' she said.

He shook his head. 'No. I'm serious. I mean it.'

She seemed to have tensed slightly. 'What are you asking, Francisco?'

'I'm asking you to marry me,' he said.

He thought her eyes brightened momentarily, and then clouded. But she said nothing; made no move; only stared at him. He waited for her to speak, but still she remained silent; silent and utterly still.

'You understand, don't you? I'm asking you to be my wife. You do understand?'

'I understand,' she said.

He took her hands in his. 'Then what do you say? Will you come to England with me?'

She gave an almost imperceptible shake of the head. 'You know I can't do that.'

'No; I don't know. Why can't you? What's to stop you?'

'You know what there is to stop me.'

'No. Tell me.'

There was another crackle of machine-gun fire. She turned her head slightly, as though listening to a strain of music.

'That?' Blade said. 'Are you telling me you can't leave that?'

'I think you are the one who does not understand,' she said.

His fingers tightened on her hands; he knew that he was hurting her, but she made no attempt to pull away.

'But you love me. Isn't that so?'

She made no answer.

'See? You can't deny it. You know it's true, don't you?'

'Perhaps.'

'Then why? In God's name, why?'

She gave a sigh. 'What good would it do if I tried to explain it? You would still not understand, because it has no meaning for you. You are not involved.'

'I'm involved with you.'

'That's something different; altogether different.'

'You bet it's different, and I'm glad it is. If I love you and you love me, Lucia, what in hell does anything else matter?'

'You just don't understand,' she said. 'You really don't.'

But she was wrong; he did understand — only too well. He understood that he was fighting a cause. He was fighting a million deprived people, to whom this girl had given herself, body and soul. Against such odds what chance did he stand?

There was another burst of firing. They were really checking those guns.

'There is an alternative,' she said. 'You know that, don't you?'

'What alternative?'

'You could come with me.'

'You mean deliver the money and then come back here?'

'It's a possibility, isn't it?'

He stared at her. 'Do you think I'm crazy? Do you think I want to spend the rest of my life being hunted by the police and the army? That's not my idea of unadulterated happiness. I've had a taste of it and the taste is sour.'

'It will not always be like that. Some day we shall win. Now that we have these arms that day may be soon.'

'Maybe. But I wouldn't like to gamble on it.'

'Not even for my sake, Francisco?'

He looked at her and thought: I'm going to hate to lose her; my God, I'm really going to hate that. He remembered that time when she had called to him from the pool, a naiad with the drops of water glistening on her skin like pearls; and the idea of leaving her, of never seeing her again, was constricting his heart.

'Is there no other way, Lucia?'

'There's no other way.'

'I'll think about it,' he said.

He could see the glitter of tears in her eyes. 'You will never come back, Francisco. You had better kiss me now. Kiss me goodbye.'

He knew it was the truth, though he hated to admit it. He kissed her, but it was not as good as it had once been; there was a bitterness in it which there had not been before. He heard more shots — one, two, three — at intervals of half a second. They were testing another rifle, another damned, bloody rifle.

'Goodbye, Francisco.'

'Goodbye, Lucia.'

## Chapter Sixteen – Money To Burn

Blade took his hired car up the gravelled winding drive to the front of Korvan's palatial house, got out, unlocked the boot, and lifted out a brand new suitcase. He had bought the suitcase because he felt that a million dollars rated something rather more sumptuous than a coarse jute sack tied up with cord; and besides, carrying a sack around tended to attract unwanted attention.

The money had come ashore in a small fishing-boat which had made a rendezvous with Svenssen's ship before any customs officers could get their undesirable hands on it and start asking awkward questions about how such a large stack of dollars came to be on board. Blade had accompanied the money and had brought it down from the remote village on the north-west coast of Scotland where the fishing-boat had put in. Everything had gone according to plan and there had been no snags. Korvan's plans had a way of turning out like that.

Blade had not yet been in touch with Korvan; he had seen no reason why he should bother to put in a telephone call and set Korvan's mind at rest. Let the bastard sweat it out for a few more days, wondering whether the cash was safe or whether his trusted agent had decided after all to do a bunk with the takings. Not that Korvan was likely to do much sweating; he was too sure of himself, too sure of his judgement of men, damn him. He would probably not even be impatient to have the money in his possession, secure in the knowledge that it would arrive in due course.

Well, it had arrived now, all safe and sound and not a dollar short. In a few minutes he would be gloating over it, starting to count it out; or maybe getting Dancey to do that for him — if he could trust Dancey to count correctly. Blade had no intention of staying any longer than was absolutely necessary; just long enough to collect his ten thousand pounds; then he would say goodbye to Korvan and hope never to see the man again.

Ten thousand pounds. Hell, it was not much in comparison with more than a million dollars. But maybe it was enough; maybe it would give him that new start he needed. If only Lucia had come with him he would have been happy enough with the ten thousand; but that part of the operation had not worked out. A pity, but that was the way things went.

The suitcase was fairly heavy with all those dollars inside it. He walked up to the big, iron-studded oak door of Korvan's house feeling weighed down on the right-hand side by this load of money. He set the case down on the doorstep and tugged at the wrought-iron bell-pull and waited.

Nothing happened; nobody opened the door; there was not a sound anywhere. He did some more work on the bell-pull and again waited. Still the door was not opened; still there was that utter silence. It was slightly eerie; he had a vague sense of misgiving, a feeling that something was wrong, that at last perhaps one of Korvan's plans had gone astray.

He tried the door. It was locked. What the devil was wrong? Had Korvan gone away? And dismissed all the staff? That was what it looked like. Yet why on earth would he go away when he was expecting delivery of a million dollars? It made no sense at all.

Blade stood on the doorstep undecided what to do next. There was no point in staying there if no one was in the house. The only sensible course of action seemed to be to go back to his room in London and try to get in touch with Korvan later. Or wait for Korvan to get in touch with him. It was a damned nuisance because it meant a further delay in completing the business, in drawing his pay and washing his hands of the whole affair; but there was no alternative. He stooped to pick up the suitcase and heard footsteps on the gravel.

It was one of the gardeners. He came to a halt and stared at Blade without recognition.

'What might you be wanting then?'

'I've been trying to get someone to answer the door,' Blade said. 'But they all seem to be asleep.'

The gardener shook his head in a slow, deliberate fashion. He was a wizened little man in a long jacket of coarse grey material.

'They ain't asleep. They ain't there.'

'Nobody?'

'Not nobody.'

'Why not?'

'Police closed the house up. They was here till yesterday, swarming all over the place, they was. Took all sorts of papers and things away, they did. Then they closed it up and went. I'm the only one as is left — caretaking like.'

It sounded ominous to Blade. So Korvan really had come unstuck at last; the police had nosed into his affairs and he had been arrested. So where did that leave him, Blade? In a pretty dodgy situation, to say the least.

But he had to get it straight. 'Why were the police here? What was the trouble?'

The wizened gardener looked surprised. 'You mean to say you ain't heard?'

'I've heard nothing. Tell me what happened.'

'Why, Mr. Korvan was murdered four days ago.'

Blade was stunned; he had certainly not been prepared for this. 'Murdered! Who murdered him?'

'Bloke named Dancey. Used to be a sort of bodyguard, so I believe.' The gardener gave a croaking laugh. 'Fine bodyguard he turned out to be. Went berserk or something. Bashed Mr. Korvan's head in. You never see such a mess; blood and brains everywhere.' The gardener seemed to be enjoying himself in a grisly kind of way; he launched into a vivid description of the scene as it had been when the servants had burst in and restrained the maddened Dancey. 'Didn't try to get away nor nothing. Just turned quiet all of a sudden like, as if he'd worked it all out of his system; as if it was something he'd been keeping bottled up for a long time and had finally got shot of, if you see what I mean.'

Blade saw what he meant. Korvan had at last goaded Dancey beyond the limits of his self-control and had paid for it with his life. And that put a very different complexion on things, very different indeed. He had to get away now and think out his next move. And the sooner the better, because there was no telling when a policeman might turn up to do a bit more nosing around. The last person he wanted to see at that moment was a policeman who might feel curious about what was inside the suitcase.

He became aware that the gardener was asking him a question: 'Are you a salesman?'

'Sort of.'

The man glanced at the suitcase. 'Brushes and that?'

'No, not brushes.'

'Well, you're wasting your time here. You won't sell him nothing. Not any more, you won't.'

'No,' Blade said, 'I don't suppose I shall.'

He put the suitcase back in the boot and locked it. He got into the hired car and drove away from Korvan's house, and he was thinking that he was never going to get that ten thousand pounds now. Never.

And then he thought of one million, one thousand and eight hundred dollars in the boot of the car, and ten thousand pounds more or less hardly seemed to matter. Because all that money was his now, every last dollar of it, every last lovely dollar.

The sun was shining and his heart was leaping and everything was fine, just fine. It was true he had not got the girl, but he had something else; he had money, money, money; money to burn. He was rich.

\*

He remained in this state of euphoria for the next twenty-four hours. Then he went to a man named Levine and tried to change one of the hundred-dollar bills. He had not gone to a bank because he was afraid the money might be hot. Banks were inclined to inform the police about little matters of that description; and he had no desire to be involved with the police, who would be bound to ask him how he had come into possession of the bill. So he went to Levine.

Levine was not a banker and he would as soon have contacted the police as an advanced case of bubonic plague; but he was a man who took nothing on trust, especially hundred-dollar bills. Therefore he examined the one that Blade had brought him with the aid of a magnifying glass; and when he had done that he pushed the bit of paper back at Blade and told him to take his phoney money somewhere else and not try to palm it off on an honest, law-abiding citizen. Which was pretty rich coming from Levine, because if he was honest and law-abiding, so too was Al Capone.

Blade was shocked. He sat on his chair in the stuffy little office at the back of the antique shop which was the legitimate front to Levine's business and stared at the hundred-dollar bill. He had thought it might well be stolen money; in fact it would not have surprised him in the least to learn that it was; but never for a moment had it occurred to him that it might not be genuine.

'You mean this is a forgery?'

Levine waggled his crowlike head at Blade. 'Are you telling me you didn't know?'

'Of course I didn't know. Would I try to pass fake money to a man like you?'

Levine treated Blade to a penetrating stare; then said: 'Well, maybe not. You'd know you hadn't a hope of getting away with it. So you did it in good faith. So that's how it is.' He lifted his narrow, bony shoulders in an expressive shrug. 'So it's no less of a fake for that. Sure, it's good counterfeit, but it's counterfeit just the same.'

Blade felt sick. Because if this hundred-dollar bill was phoney, then it was a dead certainty that all the rest of the money was too.

'You win it in a poker game, maybe?' Levine said, his beady little eyes as bright as jewels.

'Yes,' Blade said. 'A poker game.'

'You should be more careful who you play with. There's a terrible lot of dishonesty these days.'

Blade nodded. 'You can say that again.'

*

Back in his room, he opened the suitcase and stared at the money. All worthless. No wonder Lecaros had insisted on a cash deal; he had been on to a good thing — a nice big cargo of arms in exchange for a load of wastepaper. But where had he got the stuff? Did he have a press of his own and a first-rate engraver? Maybe. Not that it made any difference.

And Lucia! Had she known what kind of money it was? When she had watched him counting it in the cabin, had she known it was all a farce, a swindle? Of course she had; she must have known. But she had not told him, had not breathed a word of it. Well, that was understandable; it would have been asking for trouble. He had to be taken in; that was an essential part of the operation.

But he felt hurt, nevertheless, to think how she had cheated him. Had she been smiling inwardly all the time, even while she pretended to weep? Had she been laughing at his gullibility? No; he did not believe that; he felt sure it had given her some pain to do what she had to do. But it was no wonder that she had refused to come to England with him.

He looked at the money, at all those phoney dollars, and he had to admit that there was a funny side to the business, even if it was a sour kind of fun. Yesterday he had told himself that he had money to burn, and how right he had been! How dead bloody right!

He began to laugh. He had money to burn sure enough; one million, one thousand and eight hundred dollars of it.

He thought he would die laughing.

If you enjoyed *Final Run*, please share your thoughts on Amazon by leaving a review.

For more free and discounted eBooks every week, sign up to our newsletter.

Follow us on Twitter, Facebook and Instagram.

Printed in Great Britain
by Amazon